James G. Scott

Burma as it Was, as it Is and as it Will Be

James G. Scott

Burma as it Was, as it Is and as it Will Be

ISBN/EAN: 9783337227623

Printed in Europe, USA, Canada, Australia, Japan

Cover: Foto ©Andreas Hilbeck / pixelio.de

More available books at **www.hansebooks.com**

BURMA

AS IT WAS, AS IT IS, AND AS IT WILL BE

BY

JAMES GEORGE SCOTT

(*SHWAY YOE*)

AUTHOR OF " THE BURMAN : HIS LIFE AND NOTIONS "
" FRANCE AND TONG-KING," ETC. ETC.

LONDON
GEORGE REDWAY
YORK STREET, COVENT GARDEN
1886

PREFACE.

IT is related of a member of Parliament that some years ago he met at dinner a civilian from British Burma, home on leave. The conversation turned on that country, and the legislator remarked, " Burma—oh, yes, Burma. I had a cousin who was out there for some time, but he always called it Bermuda."

Members of Parliament now perhaps less than ever represent the intelligence and information of the country, but there is not so much known of our new province, or of our old provinces for the matter of that, as is desirable. Ordinary publicists seem to consider that a reference to " pestilential swamps " is the most vivid way of giving an idea of what the country is like.

A sketch of the country, of its history, and of its industrial prospects will therefore not be considered out of place.

In writing this book the author has followed the lines of, and utilized to some extent, a lecture delivered before the Society of Arts in January 1886. The most recent authorities have throughout been consulted, including the Parliamentary Blue-Book of 1886. The author is also particularly indebted for the sketch of the Burmese Constitution to a lecture delivered at Simla, before the United Service Institute, by Mr. R. H. Pilcher, of the Burma Commission.

CONTENTS.

CONTENTS.

BURMA:

AS IT WAS, AS IT IS, AND AS IT WILL BE.

—·•·—

I.—THE HISTORY.

BURMA ACCORDING TO NATIVE THEORIES.

THE Burmese system of the universe is very orderly, but it conflicts somewhat with the theories of Western men of science. In the centre stands Mount Meru, shaped like a cask floating end upwards, half above the ocean, half below. It rests on three feet, huge rubies and carbuncles. On its slopes are the six seats of Devas, the beings who, by good works and incessant meditation, have risen above man's estate on the path to Nirvana. Above the mountain in the empyrean are the sixteen seats of the Brahmas, the Perfect, who live in a state

B

oɪ sublime contemplation. Down below are the eight great hells and the numberless smaller ones. Round Mount Meru extends the vast Thamohddaya ocean, girdled in by the seven ranges of the Sekyawala hills, with seven seas interposed. In the sea round Mount Meru are four great islands—the northern, eastern, southern, and western— and each of these has five hundred small islands round about it. The race of man inhabits the southern island. The Burmese, the Chinese and Indo-Chinese, and the Indians people the mainland, and the English and other foreigners live in the small islands.

The eastern, western, and northern islands are very pleasant to live in, but especially the northern. It is a regular land of Cockayne. Gorgeous dresses hang ready-made from the trees. Dainty meats of all kinds grow up and cook themselves. But still they are not happy. Like the eastern and western islanders, they are always reborn in the same place, and cannot raise themselves. It is only in the southern island that Buddhas appear to teach the law, and free the people from constant deaths and reappearances. Only there can man rise in the scale of existence, until he finally frees himself from passion, and sorrow, and the trammels of existence, and sinks into the bliss of Nirvana. Therefore, the pious have called the southern island the ferry to Nirvana.

The whole universe is destroyed once in an Asankya,

> "which is the tale
> Of all the drops that in ten thousand years
> Would fall on all the worlds by daily rain."

The present universe, called Badda, has a little over four quadrillion years to run.

It was first peopled by Brahmas, nine inhabitants of the highest Buddhist heavens, who came down and settled upon earth. At first they lived upon a particular kind of flavoured earth, but gradually they became tired of this, and took to eating the seeds of a species of creeper, even as Adam and Eve ate the forbidden fruit. Thus they became gradually less and less spiritual and more and more material, until at last they lost all their heavenly attributes, and had to live by the sweat of their brow like all their

descendants.   From these Brahmas, the
Burmese claim to be the lineal descendants.
They call themselves Bam-ma.   This word
is written Myam-ma, and used to be pronounced Byam-ma, and this is obviously,
according to the national idea of etymology,
the same thing as Brahma.   The theory
reminds one of Pope Gregory's "*Non Angli,
sed angeli.*"   The Burmese are not mere
Burmans ; they are celestial beings.   They
are no more angelic now than, it is painful
to admit, latter-day or even ancient Britons,
but at any rate the claim is one which should
meet with English sympathy, especially as
the   Burman   is   the   most   genial   of   all
Orientals.   Philologists, it is true, who have
the   modern   mania   for   spoiling   pretty
stories, declare that this is all wrong.   They
assert that Myam-ma is only a mutilated
form of Myo-ma.   *Myo* means "people" or
"race," and the Burmans would therefore
be, not fallen angels, but simply men—
emphatically *men* certainly, but still only
men.   In proof of this, the Mro, a hill-tribe
now existing in our Arakan province, are
pointed out as a living demonstration of the
fact.   Therefore the Brahma theory must

probably be abandoned, just as it is impossible for us to accept Mount Meru and the seven encircling seas. If the Burmans are not the descendants of celestial beings, they may hope to become celestial beings themselves in a future existence.

The particular part of the southern island they inhabit is called the Ashay Pyee, the Eastern Country. The Chinese live east of them, it is true; but the Chinese are "elder brothers" and Buddhists, though very bad ones. India is called the Middle Country. The east is the place of honour, for it was from the east that the Buddha came. The name has, therefore, the signification of the "foremost country," the one that is superior to all others, the country ruled over by the King of the Umbrella-bearing Chiefs, the Arbiter of Existence, the great Lord of Righteousness, as the King of Burma was called, among other titles.

This conviction not only of their own superiority, but of the superiority of their country over all others, has had a great influence on the Burmese character, both in their estimation of themselves and in the attitude which they have adopted towards foreign

nations. It has been fostered by their literature, and Buddhism itself has done not a little
to strengthen the assurance that they, with
their heavenly descent, and their kings of the
true solar race, are indeed in the foremost
ranks of time.

ORIGIN OF THE BURMESE.

Now that we have got the Burmese notions
of themselves, we may turn to more matter-of-
fact statements about the people and the
country. There is a multitude of tribes in
all parts of the land called by the general
name of Burma, having different names, a
great variety of customs and religion, and
considerable dialectic diversities. But a
closer examination shows that there are
really only four main groups :—

The Burmans proper, who, broadly speaking, inhabit the newly annexed province;

The Talaings or Môns, who occupy the
delta provinces and are frequently referred
to as Peguans;

The Karenns, who are found in the country
round about Toung-oo and in the hills
between the Salween and Sittang rivers;

Finally, the Shans, who are the most extensively diffused and probably the most numerous of the Indo-Chinese races, lapping both Upper and Lower Burma round from the north-west by the north and east to the south-west, extending from Assam down to Bangkok and farther east to Camboja and almost to Tong-King.

It is an undecided question where the Burmese came from, but everything seems to point to the south-eastern border of the great Central Asian table-land. All the rivers draining northern Indo-China rise in the Eastern Himalayas, and no road is so easy for an emigrating nation as the valley of a river. It is also quite certain that the Môn or Talaing people are simply earlier wanderers from the same original dwelling-places as the Burmese. The Talaing language, whether in its written or spoken form, is quite incomprehensible to a Burman, but it has almost entirely died out within the last fifty years, and once more the Upper and Lower Burmans speak the same language. In general appearance there never has been any marked distinction, except that the Talaings were somewhat lighter-coloured than the

Burmans. Both in physiognomy and language they are obviously Tartars and akin to the Bhotiyas, the tribes of Tibet and of the vast steppes of High Asia. In figure they are short and thickset, with high cheek-bones, and slightly projecting jaw, and the flat face which is unmistakably Mongolian. There is but very little of the Chinese tilt of the eye. In colour they vary from the tint of a wax-candle to that of a dead oak-leaf, accordingly as they belong to the leisured town-classes or to the workers in the rice-fields. Both men and women have long black hair, not unseldom three or four feet in length, and they are very proud of it. The men wear it tied in a knot on the top of the head and encircled by the turban ; the women, in a chignon at the back. Both sexes are fond of bulking out this knot with false tresses. The men tattoo breeches on themselves, from the waist to below the knee, with sessamum-seed soot. The figures traced are ogres, tigers, monkeys, spirits, and each is surrounded by a border of mysterious cabalistic letters, while magic squares and lucky marks are also commonly introduced. Vermilion figures are also tattooed on the chest and arms and back with special superstitious purposes. The women are not tattooed. The origin of the custom, of which the people are very proud, is very obscure. The Arakanese, it may be mentioned, are undoubtedly Burmese, and the unimportant differences of dialect are due to the neighbourhood of Bengal and to the range of hills which separates them from the main body of the race. The Talaing language, on the contrary, is the most isolated in its character of all Indo-China. Its roots are not allied to any of the surrounding languages, whether of Farther India or China. A resemblance has, it is thought, been traced with the vocables of the Kols and other Central Indian tribes. The language is, however, as already re-marked, fast dying out.

The Karenns, on the other hand, are cer-tainly not of the same race as either Burmans or Talaings, and it is equally without doubt that they are not the aborigines of the coun-try. They have no written character of their own, and they did not adopt Buddhism, so that their traditions are very ancient and singular. Among them are some remarkable suggestions of Old Testament history, even to the extent of an account of the Deluge

and of the names of Adam and Eve. Therefore they have inevitably been identified with
the lost ten tribes. They claim to have come
from the north, and the " river of sand "
which their ancestors crossed seems to point
to the Desert of Gobi. On the other hand,
other traditions unquestionably refer to China,
and have suggested an identity with the Miau-
tsŭ, as the Chinese call some of their hill-tribes.
The probability is that they migrated several
times before finally settling down as the subjects of the Burmese and Talaings. They are
much gentler in their manner than their
neighbours, and great numbers have of late
years been converted to Christianity.

The Shans, we are told by Mons. Terrien
de Lacouperie, originally came from the
western part of the Chinese province of Such'uen, and are the elder brothers of the
Siamese. There are comparatively few of
them under our rule, but it may be hoped
they will not delay to flock down into the
fertile lowlands, for they are as fine agriculturists as the Chinese themselves. They are
split up into a great number of disconnected
principalities, some nominally subject to
Burma, some to Siam, but they are a very

fine race. Everywhere they are Buddhists, and that is the most tolerant of non-Christian faiths, and everywhere they are civilized, and possess more or less of a literature. They are probably destined to become our most industrious subjects and most satisfactory neighbours.

EARLY HISTORY.

All the early history, both that which the Burmese adopted with Buddhism and the portion which is founded on national legends, may be dismissed as more or less imaginative, a kind of "Arabian Nights" of a somewhat truculent kind. The entirely legendary portion ends in the seventh or eighth century before our era, and the fairy-tale history then begins. It is unnecessary to refer to any portion of it before the days of the great Venetian traveller. Already in the time of Ser Marco Polo, the Burmese were a formidable power. The old Venetian writes :—

" Now there was [in A.D. 1272] a certain King of Mien [the Chinese name for Burma] and Bengala who was a very puissant prince, with much territory, and treasure, and people, and he was not yet subject to the great Khan [Emperor of China], though it was not long after that the latter conquered him, and took from him both kingdoms which I have named. And it came to pass when the King of Mien and Bengala heard that the host of the great Khan was at Vochan [the present Yung-Chang], he said to himself that it behoved him to go against them with so great a force as would ensure his cutting off the whole of them. So this king prepared a great force and ammunitions of war, and he had 2000 great elephants, on each of which was set a tower of timber, well bound and strong, and carrying twelve to sixteen fighting-men. When the king had completed these great preparations to fight the Tartars, he tarried not, but marched straight against them. And after marching without meeting with anything worth mentioning, they arrived within three days of the great Khan's host, which was then at Vochan in Zardandan, so there he pitched his camp. And when the captain of the Tartar host, Nasaradin, had certain news of the aforesaid king, he waxed

uneasy, as he had with him but 12,000 horse-
men. However, he advanced to receive the
enemy in the plain of Vochan, and when the
king's army had arrived in the plain, and was
within a mile of the enemy, he caused all the
elephants to be ordered for battle, and began
to advance. The horses of the Tartars took
so much fright at the sight of the elephants,
that they would not face the foe. And when
the Tartars perceived how the case stood,
they were in great wrath. But their captain
acted like a wise leader, for he ordered every
man to dismount, and to tie his horse to a
tree, and then to take their bows. They did
as he bade them, and plied their bows so
stoutly on the advancing elephants, that in a
short space they had wounded or slew the
greatest part of them. So when the elephants felt the smart of the arrows that
pelted them like rain, they turned and fled
into the woods, dashing their castles against
the trees, and bruising the warriors. So
when the Tartars saw that the elephants had
turned tail, they got to horse, and at once
charged the enemy, and then the battle raged
furiously, and when they had continued
fighting till midday, the king's troops

would stand against the Tartars no longer,
but felt they were defeated, and turned
and fled."

Immediately after this came the first
Chinese invasion of Burma. The king
retreated on the sea-coast, and his capital,
Pagán on the Irrawaddy, was sacked. The
Chinese, however, after a time, retired over
the hills again. After this there were periodic
invasions from China, most of them unsuc-
cessful, but the result was that Burma was
split up into separate kingdoms—Pegu, the
Talaing kingdom, Arakan, and Upper Burma,
the country of the Burmese proper, with
occasional independent kings in particular
districts such as Toung-oo.

FIRST APPEARANCE OF EUROPEANS IN BURMA.

It is only after the Portuguese navigators
entered the eastern seas that any real notion
of the actual state of Burma can be formed.
Malacca was captured by Albuquerque in
1511, and at that time it would seem that the
country now known as Burma was divided
into four kingdoms—Arakan, Pegu, Burma,

and Ava, each having its own king, and quarrelling with its neighbours. One of these, Buyin-Gyee Noung Zaw, or Branginoco, as he is called by the old chroniclers, engaged a number of Portuguese adventurers, and with their aid subdued his neighbours, and even invaded Siam. He was murdered, as most Sovereigns were in those days, and succeeding kings in all the kingdoms round about in succession engaged Portuguese soldiers of fortune, and invaded and ravaged and slaughtered vigourosly.

At last, in 1600, the King of Arakan gave the port of Syriam, close to Rangoon, to Philip de Brito, better known as Nicote, one of the most notable of these soldiers of fortune. This seems to have been the first concession of land in Burma to any European Power, and it speedily excited a desire for more. Nicote went off to Goa and obtained six ships of war to effect the conquest of Pegu. This he partially succeeded in doing, and it was only after thirteen years' nearly continuous fighting that Syriam was taken and Nicote impaled. About the same time another adventurer, Gonsalves, a Spaniard, established himself on the island of Sunda in the Sunderbunds, and waged war on Moguls and Arakanese alike. But he and his followers were mere pirates, and, at the price of vassalage to the King of Portugal, the Arakanese monarch received assistance from the Viceroy of Goa, and extirpated them. But the suzerainty was only slightly acknowledged. The other potentates made Portuguese alliances also, and constant wars went on without advantage to any one.

Our connection with Burma began about the same time, and was certainly more peaceful. Mr. Ralph Fitch seems to have been the first Englishman who visited Burma. He was there in 1586, and his objects were more commercial than warlike. In his narrative he tells us that the city of Pegu was "strong, very fair, with walls of stone, and great ditches round about it." It had twenty gates, was built square, and the moat was full of crocodiles, which reminds one of the way in which the kings of Annam defended their treasury. The town was very rich and populous, and, notwithstanding the constant wars, did much trade. Opium is specially mentioned, so that we are hardly so guilty in that matter as some people would have us believe. Masulipatam sent painted cloth, and Bengal its

"Turkises, 'evening-sky' tint, woven webs
So fine twelve folds hide not a modest face."

Cotton, sandal, porcelain, and other wares came from China, camphor from Borneo, pepper from Atchín in Sumatra. European goods were sent from Mecca—woollen cloths, velvets, scarlets, and the like. The exports were mostly metals, gold and silver, sapphires and rubies, musk, lacquer, wax, rice, and sugar. Altogether, Ralph Fitch's account is a relief after the continual massacreings and impalings of the Portuguese.

The result was considerable trade with Burma from both England and Holland. In the early part of the seventeenth century both English and Dutch had factories at Bhamô, north of Mandalay. The Dutch, however, quarrelled with the Burmese, and threatened to call in the Chinese to their aid. The Burmese then, as now, were little inclined to yield to threats, and they turned the Dutch out of the country, and the English along with them. The Dutch were never re-admitted, and it was many years before we were either.

C

At last, however, in 1697, a Mr. Thomas Bowyer arrived in Syriam, and a factory was established, only to be burnt down because Mr. Smart, the East India Company's agent of the time, mixed himself up in the quarrels of the Burmese and the Talaings. This was in 1743, and led to the withdrawal of the establishment about forty-six years after it had been founded.

Meanwhile, the turn of Fortune's wheel had brought the Peguans to the top. They invaded Burma, sacked and burnt Ava, and carried the king off as a prisoner, and, after keeping him in confinement some time, put him in a red sack and drowned him in the river. Notwithstanding that this was strictly in accordance with precedent, the Burmese were so enraged that they rose and massacred the Talaing garrisons, and eventually gathering round a simple hunter of the small village of Myouk-myo, or Moht-sho-bo, eighty miles north-west of Ava, not only expelled the Talaings, but pursued them into their own country and conquered Pegu and Tenasserim and eventually Arakan. At last, in 1757, their leader built a palace at Dagohn and called the place Yan-gohn — the war is finished. This is Rangoon, the present capital of Burma, for we are hardly likely to shift the seat of government to Mandalay, and the warlike hunter was Aloung-payah, or Alompra as he is usually called, the founder of the last Burmese dynasty.

FRENCH INTRIGUES IN BURMA AND THE CHINESE SUZERAINTY THEORY.

Alompra united the whole country under his rule, and, as there was now some chance of making a treaty which would not be upset by local disturbances, both the East India Company and Dupleix, the Governor-General of French India, were soon busy asking for favours. The king gave Negrais island, also called Hain-gyee, on the Arakan coast, to the British in perpetuity, and allowed the French to keep on a factory at Syriam. Neither settlement, however, was destined to last long. Alompra was informed that the Syriam traders were intriguing with the Peguans, and about the same time, in 1759, the French were killed or carried prisoners to Ava, and the English on Hain-gyee were massacred, all but a few who were able to escape to the ships in the offing. Captain Alves was sent to demand satisfaction, for there were some soldiers among the victims, but, when he reached Ava, he found that Alompra was dead and the city in rebellion. The great king died on an expedition against Siam. He had demanded a daughter of the royal house in marriage, and, when she was refused, marched off to fetch her. But he died before he could do it, after seven years' reign.

No satisfaction was got for the Negrais massacre, notwithstanding that three years later Sin-Byoo-Shin (the Lord of the White Elephant), the second son of Alompra, established himself firmly on the throne. We had more serious matters on hand in India then. Sin-Byoo-Shin reigned thirteen years, and during all that time he was fighting. He repulsed four invasions of the Chinese, who wanted to exact tribute. He invaded Siam, destroyed Ayuthia, the then capital, and took most of the royal family prisoners. He asserted his authority over the Shan States as far as the Mekong, and he overran and practically annexed Munnipur.

The reign of Sin-Byoo-Shin is particularly

important, because it was in his time that
were established the relations between
Burma and China which have lasted down
to the present day. With one single exception (in the middle of the seventeenth century),
the Chinese had shown no disposition to
interfere in the affairs of Burma for a period of
four hundred years. In 1765, however, war
broke out, owing to the ill-treatment of some
Chinese traders. Four successive Chinese
armies were sent into Burma, and, as has
been stated, they were all defeated. The
Chinese contention is that they were only
routed in the Burmese history-books, and
that, as a matter of fact, Burma was forced
to pay tribute then, and has done so ever
since. But this assertion the Burmese
equally sturdily deny, and refer to the
following treaty in proof of it. The text
is as given by Professor Douglas :—

"Wednesday, December 13, 1769, in the
temporary building to the south-east of the
town of Kaung-tun, His Excellency the
General of the Lord who rules over the
multitude of umbrella-wearing chiefs in the
Western Kingdom, the Sun-descended King

of Ava, and Master of the Golden Palace, having appointed [here follow the names and titles of the fourteen Burmese officers], and the generals of the Master of the Golden Palace of China, who rules over a multitude of umbrella-wearing chiefs in the great Eastern Kingdom, having appointed [here follow the names and titles of the thirteen Chinese officers], they assembled in the large building erected in the proper manner with seven roofs, to the south-east of the town of Kaung-tun, on December 13, 1769, to negotiate peace and friendship between the two great countries, and that the gold and silver road should be established agreeably to former custom. The troops of the Sun-descended King and Master of the Golden Palace of Ava, and those of the Master of the Golden Palace of China, were drawn up in front of each other when these negotiations took place; and, after its conclusion, each party made presents to the other, agreeably to former custom, and retired. All men, the subjects of the Sun-descended King and Master of the Golden Palace of Ava, who may be in any part of the dominions of the Master of the Golden Palace of China, shall be treated according to former custom. Peace

and friendship being established between the
two great countries, they shall become one,
like two pieces of gold united into one; and
suitably to the establishment of the gold and
silver road, as well as agreeably to former
custom, the princes and officers of each country shall move their respective Sovereigns to
transmit and exchange affectionate letters on
gold, once every ten years."

The Chinese historians make no mention
of anything more than a formal agreement,
for it would of course put an end to all idea
of suzerainty if they admitted the conclusion
of a regular treaty, and they lay great stress
on the letters and presents sent every ten
years. But, as a matter of history, China
was the first to send a mission, and it is
equally certain that, ever since, Burma has
retained at least a nominal lordship over
Shan States previously included in the
Chinese Empire. The Emperor K'ien-
lung's letter was written as to an equal
except that, throughout, the title "elder
brother" was applied to himself. The
presents sent periodically were referred to
as tribute in the *Peking Gazette*, but it is
a matter of sufficient notoriety that Great

Britain has been recorded in that venerable and veracious sheet as being tributary to the great Hwang-ti. The Chinese claim to the fealty of Burma will therefore not bear investigation. In the countries where China has really exercised a suzerainty she has always taken care to make this manifest, by allowing no one to reign without confirmation of his title from the vermilion pencil. It is not pretended that this right was ever exercised in the instance of a single one of the princes of the House of Alompra. A special embassy always came from Peking to enthrone the kings of Annam. Communications between Burma and China have always been fitful. No Burman king thought it necessary to announce his succession to the "elder brother," and even the stipulated decennial letters were not always sent. It is quite certain that no direct communication has passed between Mandalay and Peking since 1875, and that was four years before King Theebaw succeeded to the throne. The interchanges of missions had no other meaning than the fostering of a trade which was profitable to both countries. Complimentary letters and presents are among the commonplaces of Oriental intercourse. It may be confidently asserted that China's claim to suzerainty over Burma is all fudge. The *Peking Gazette*, in its translation, represented the Burman letter as using the language of a superior to an inferior. The Burman *Than-daw-zin*, when he read the Emperor of China's epistle aloud before the king, similarly modified that document. It is urged that the Chinese envoys were always minor officials, such as would not be sent to an independent Power, according to Oriental etiquette. But this argument applies equally to the Burmese officials. On no recorded occasion was a *Woon-gyee*, a Minister of the highest rank, sent. The bearers of the letter of gold and the presents were *Than-daw-zins*, the ordinary royal heralds, or at the most *Woon-dauks*, officers of fourth or fifth rank. It is no doubt highly desirable for the political and commercial prosperity of Burma that we should be on cordial terms with China, but it would be equally unwise and impolitic to recognize suzerain rights which, if they ever existed at all, date from the time of the early Manchus, and have no existence in modern times except in the brains of plenipotentiaries who qualify a knowledge of musty old records with a smattering of Western international usages. No one would combat the Chinese claims with greater vigour than the Burmese themselves. There is no reason why we should be more foolishly complaisant.

WORRYING OUR REPRESENTATIVES.

After the death of Sin-Byoo-Shin there was a great deal of quarrelling over the succession, and two kings and any number of conspiring princes were sewn up in red sacks and thrown into the Irrawaddy. At last, however, in 1782, Bo-daw Payah (the sainted royal grandfather) succeeded, and with him, in 1795, we first came into direct political intercourse. Captain Symes was sent by Sir John Shore, the Governor-General of India, on an embassy to Ava for the purpose of strengthening our commercial relations and preventing the French from gaining a footing in the country. In addition to this, the Burmese, who had meanwhile annexed Arakan, had been making hostile demonstrations on our Chittagong frontier. Symes' mission was not very successful, but he obtained a royal order, granting permission for the establishment of a British residency at Rangoon. Captain Hiram Cox was sent to act as agent in 1796, but he was subjected to so many indignities, both in Rangoon and Ava, that he returned to Calcutta. But there was much unpleasantness between English merchant-skippers and the Rangoon native authorities, so in 1802 Captain Symes was again sent to the Burmese capital by Lord Wellesley. The mission was a grand one, and Symes was ordered to seek a treaty of alliance and to demand the recession of Negrais island, or compensating commercial advantages. The fate of Martin da Costa Falcom, the Portuguese ambassador of the seventeenth century, awaited him. The mission was an utter failure. The gallant captain never had a proper audience. He was persistently and elaborately insulted, and eventually went back to Bengal without settling anything. But the Indian Government was not daunted, and many efforts at negotiation were made afterwards. The story is, however, not a pleasant one, and I only refer to the matter to show that French intrigue is no new matter in Burma, and that Burmese officials have been consistently overbearing and contemptuous, while we, through our representatives, have been patient and long-suffering. The insolent treatment of our envoys was not our only cause of complaint. Wherever Burmese territory touched British there was aggression, and no redress was to be had. The king demanded the surrender of refugees who had fled into our territory for protection, and, when this was refused, called upon the Governor-General to cede Chittagong, Dacca, and Murshidabad.

WAR WITH BURMA.

There could be only one end to this, and it came in 1825. The Burmese drove a sepoy garrison out of Supari island at the mouth of the Naaf river, and we declared war. At this time the empire of Burma was one of the most extensive, as well as the most formidable, powers in Asia. Besides Burma proper, and the provinces of Pegu, Arakan, and Tenasserim, it embraced the principality of Mogoung, the northern Shan and Kachyen States, Assam, Cachar, and Munnipur, and had as tributaries all the Shan chieftains as far as the Mékong river. It had a thousand miles of sea-board, and years of constant fighting had made a naturally brave and warlike people so confident in their invincibility that they listened complacently to the order of the day issued, calling upon them to march to England. The first fighting began in Sylhet and Assam, and there our troops were held in check for some time, while in Chittagong they were routed by a superior force of Burmese. Calcutta was in a state of panic, and the Europeans formed themselves into a militia. Then, however, the capture of Rangoon by a British force, and the defeat of the Burmese generals there, caused a diversion, and Assam and Chittagong were evacuated by the Burmese. It is not necessary to give an account of the war. The British force numbered only a little over 12,000, of whom about 7,000 belonged to native regiments, but they were enough, notwithstanding the determination with which the Burmese fought on several occasions, especially under their great general, Mahah Bundoola. Eventually in 1826, after a battle at Pagán, when the English troops under Sir

Archibald Campbell were at Yandabo, only forty-five miles from Ava, the king gave in. Arakan, Tenasserim, and a part of Martaban were ceded to us. Cachar, Jyntea, and Assam were given up, and Munnipur was declared independent and under British protection. The terms were cheap, for the country was entirely at our mercy. The expedition had been begun at the worst time of year, and Burmese duplicity delayed our troops several times in most feverish jungles. The consequence was that the losses of our troops were enormous. During the two years of the war the mortality amounted to 72.5 per cent. of the men engaged, and of these only 5 per cent. were killed in action. This has never been forgotten, and to this day one hears of the pestilential swamps and the dreadful climate of Burma. As a matter of fact, it is as healthy as, if not more healthy than, most parts of India.

The Burmese had got a lesson, but they did not profit much by it. The king and his governors were as insolent and contemptuous as ever. Major Burney stayed for some years as Resident at Ava, but the insults which were offered became so constant and unendurable that he asked and obtained permission from the Indian Government to withdraw, and his example was followed by several successors. The state of affairs cannot be better described than in Lord Dalhousie's words :—

" Of all the Eastern natives with which the Government of India has had to do, the Burmese are the most arrogant and overbearing. During the years since the [1826] treaty had been concluded, they had treated it with disregard, and had been allowed to disregard it with impunity. They had been permitted to 'worry away' our envoys by petty annoyances, and their insolence had even been tolerated when at last they vexed our commercial agent at Rangoon into silent departure from their port. Inflated by such indirect successes as these, the Burmese had assumed again the tone they used before the war of 1825. On more than one occasion they had threatened a recommencement of hostilities against us, and always at the most untoward time. Every effort was made to obtain reparation by friendly means. The reparation was no more than compensation for the actual loss incurred, but every effort was in vain. Our demands were evaded, our officers were insulted. The warnings which we gave were treated with disregard, and the period of grace which we allowed was employed by the Burmese in strengthening their fortifications and in making every preparation for resistance."

It is as well to insist on this, because those good people who always maintain that the man who fights is in the wrong, declare that we had not sufficient grounds for the second Burmese War of 1852. It began suddenly, and it was finished drastically. We drove the Burmese troops out of Martaban, Rangoon, Bassein, Pegu, Toung-oo, and Prome, the townspeople everywhere receiving us as friends. From this last town we might have advanced by steam on Ava, as General Prendergast did in 1885. But Lord Dalhousie determined to rest content with the province of Pegu, in compensation for the past and for better security in the future. No treaty was entered into with the king, who indeed had been deposed by his own subjects. The country was simply taken possession of, and a proclamation to that effect was issued and peace declared in 1853.

THE INEVITABLE END.

King Mindohn, who was on the throne of Burma at the close of the second Burmese War, was probably the best king Burma ever had—certainly the best of the Alompra dynasty. Nevertheless, it may be stated broadly that the regular diplomatic representation of the British Government at the Burmese Court, which had been suspended in 1839, was not resumed till 1862. Sir Arthur Phayre then negotiated a treaty, and left an Agent at Mandalay. This treaty provided that British traders should be allowed to travel over the whole Upper Irrawaddy, and make what purchases they chose. A corresponding provision guaranteed free travel and trade to Burmese traders along the Irrawaddy in British territory. But the treaty did not work well, for, though the British Government abolished certain customs duties on its side of the frontier, the Burmese indefinitely postponed performance of their part of the agreement.

D

At the same time, the royal monopolies (for his Majesty had turned into a gigantic trader) operated greatly in restraint of the development of trade.

These were to a great degree restricted by the treaty of 1867, concluded by General Fytche. The Mandalay Government was also pledged for ten years to several valuable commercial arrangements, while at the same time the 1862 treaty remained in full force. The British Resident in Mandalay received civil jurisdiction over cases in which British subjects were concerned, and a Political Agency was established at Bhamô, near the Chinese frontier. Nevertheless, our relations with Upper Burma remained incomplete, unsatisfactory, and ill-assured. The 1867 treaty lapsed in 1877, and was not renewed. There were disputes about territorial matters, such as the interference of the Burmese in Western Karennee and encroachment on our Arakan frontier, and above all there was the hampering of diplomatic intercourse by the great "shoe-question." Our representative was not allowed to see the king except in his stocking-soles and seated on the floor, and all attempts to obtain the abandonment of this absurd and humiliating ceremonial were in vain.

Things were in this unsatisfactory state when King Theebaw succeeded to the throne, in October 1878. He owed his position to a Court intrigue, for his father had not intended him to ascend the throne, and, indeed, there were strong doubts as to his legitimacy. There was some hope that the new king might attempt to strengthen his position by commencing better relations with us, especially as his accession was accompanied by the announcement that he was going to institute constitutional government. So far from this being the case, King Theebaw's dislike to a British alliance proved more violent than his father's. British subjects were put in the stocks, these were hoisted to the roof, and the victims were suspended for hours by their ankles. British steamers were stopped, and forcible seizures made on board of them ; and finally, four months after his accession, occurred the infamous Palace massacres which have made the king's name so notorious. Our Resident remonstrated against these atrocities in very strong language, but received no more satisfactory reply than the cynical statement that such "clearing-away" matters must remain at the discretion of any independent Government. Eventually, so insolent and menacing did the attitude of both Ministers and people become towards the Resident that, in October 1879, the Government of India considered it prudent to withdraw our Agency with all its *personnel.*

Triumphant over this success, the Burmese Government now grew more openly hostile. Several unprovoked attacks were made on the captains and crews of British mail-steamers lying at anchor in the river, and demands for redress were so ill-received that the renunciation of all treaty engagements with King Theebaw was contemplated. Then his Majesty tried a new line. An official of low rank was sent down with a draft treaty, but the articles were found to be so inadmissible—a demand for unlimited power of importing material of war being the main item—and the king's overtures were so evidently insincere and illusory, that the envoy was not allowed to proceed beyond our frontier. Immediately after his return to Mandalay he died, and it was asserted that he was poisoned by the king's command.

The relations between the two Governments remained at a dead-lock. Fresh massacres took place in the capital; bands of robbers infested the country, and raided at will into British territory; the greater part of the tributary Shan States rose in rebellion, and the whole of Upper Burma became disorganized, with the inevitable result of a paralysis of our trade. Upper and Lower Burma are naturally one country. The boundary was a mere arbitrary line drawn along a parallel of latitude, with masonry pillars, half hid in the jungle, to mark it. Consequently, the anarchy and misrule beyond the frontier made themselves very painfully felt in our lower provinces. In the midst of all this, King Theebaw, in 1882, sent a new envoy with fresh proposals for a treaty. Notwithstanding the state of affairs and the vague nature of the proposals, Lord Ripon received the ambassador in the most friendly way, and was prepared to go to any length to procure a settlement. But, in the middle of the negotiations, King Theebaw suddenly changed his mind and recalled his envoy,

There is good reason to believe that these so-called ambassadors were simply spies, sent to see how we were disposed towards the Court of Mandalay.

After this, however, the king's envoys went elsewhere. The policy of menace and hostility showed itself in the despatch of missions to Europe seeking alliances with France and Italy for the purpose of attaining political and commercial arrangements which, considering the position of Burma, we could not possibly tolerate. The French signed nothing more than a commercial treaty, but there can be no doubt that the aim of the Burmese was to obtain from the French Government such a treaty as would enable them to appeal to France in case of their being involved in difficulties with England; or, in fact, that their great object, in forming relations with European Powers, was to find means of emancipating themselves from the special influence and control of the Indian Government. As long as Upper Burma occupied an isolated position we could afford to submit to much insolence and provocation, but when the king embarked upon an external policy of this kind it was obviously impossible to forbear any longer. It would have been extremely dangerous to have allowed the possibility of a quarrel being raised with Burma on a clause of a treaty between that country and France. The Republic, as usual, had its over-zealous agents, and one of these gentlemen, the French consul in Mandalay, Mons. Haas, obtained sanction to make several proposals to his Government. These were : the construction of a railway from Mandalay to Toung-oo, on our frontier ; the control by a French company over the levy of customs duties on the Irrawaddy ; a monopoly of pickled tea, an anti-soporific dainty largely consumed in the lower provinces ; and, finally, the establishment by a Frenchman of a royal bank. Now, India dominates Burma so entirely that we could not permit this practical handing over of the country to a foreign Power, with the probable eventual result of the neutralization of Burma and the opening up of the Irrawaddy to vessels of all nations on some such footing as the Danube now is denationalized.

While yet it was under consideration how this danger should be faced, there occurred a matter which left no choice but prompt and

decided action.   King Theebaw, instigated
no doubt by Mons. Haas, attempted to im-
pose a preposterous and ruinous fine on the
Bombay Burma Trading Corporation, and
followed up this by a threat of confiscation
of the whole of their valuable property in
default of payment.   The alleged grounds
for the fine were wholly ridiculous.   The
Government of India proposed that the matter in dispute should go before an arbitrator.
This the king's Government peremptorily
refused, and declared the matter definitely
settled.   Thereupon an ultimatum was sent
to Mandalay demanding the arrangement of
the general relations of the two countries on
a satisfactory footing; and this was accompanied by a warning that, in the event of
these proposals not being accepted, Britain
would take the matter into her own hands.
The answer was the following declaration of
war by King Theebaw, dated November 7,
1885 :—

"To all town and village thugyees, heads of
cavalry, heads of the Daings, shield bearers,
heads of jails, heads of gold and silver
revenues, mine workers, settlement officers,

heads of forests, and to all royal subjects and inhabitants of the royal empire :

" Those heretics, the English kalás [barbarians], having most harshly made demands calculated to bring about the impairment and destruction of our religion, the violation of our national traditions and customs, and the degradation of our race, are making a show and preparation as if about to wage war with our State. They have been replied to in conformity with the usages of great nations, and in words which are just and regular. If, notwithstanding, these heretic kalás should come and in any way attempt to molest or disturb the State, his Majesty, who is watchful that the interests of our religion and our State shall not suffer, will himself march forth with his generals, captains, and lieutenants, with large forces of infantry, artillery, elephanterie, and cavalry, by land and by water, and with the might of his army will efface these heretic kalás and conquer and annex their country. All royal subjects the people of the country are enjoined that they are not to be alarmed or disturbed on account of the hostility of these heretic kalás, and they are not to avoid them by quitting the country.

"They are to continue to carry on their occupations as usual in a peaceful and ordinary manner; the local officials are to be watchful, each in his own town or village, that it is free from thefts, dacoities, and other crime; the royal troops to be sent forth will not be collected and banded together as formerly by forcibly pressing into service all such as can be obtained, but the royal troops who are now already banded into regiments in Mandalay will be sent forth to attack, destroy, and annex. The local officials shall not forcibly impress into service any one who may not wish to serve. To uphold the religion, to uphold the national honour, to uphold the country's interests, will bring about threefold good : good of our religion, good of our master, and good of ourselves; and will gain for us the important result of placing us in the path to the celestial regions and to Nehban Nirvana. Whoever, therefore, is willing to join and serve zealously will be assisted by his Majesty with royal rewards and royal money, and be made to serve in the capacity for which he may be fit. Loyal officials are to make inquiries for volunteers and others who may wish to serve, and are to submit lists of them to their respective provincial governments."

Order of the Ministers of the Hlohtdaw. Names follow. On the 7th of November 1885. Burmese date recorded by the Wetmasoht Woondauk Daw, issued by Secretary Mah Mindin Minhla Sithu.

On the last day of the same month King Theebaw was a prisoner in our hands. Our clemency had lasted long enough. We might have annexed in 1826, or in 1853; we have done so in 1886. There was no other possible end to the question.

II.—THE COUNTRY.

LOWER BURMA.

LOWER BURMA, as it may be called for the sake of distinction, seeing that the former title of British Burma is now inadequate, is, like ancient Gaul, divided into three parts—the provinces of Arakan, Pegu, and Tenasserim ; and the three together are as nearly as possible equal in area to Great Britain and Ireland—94,000 square miles is the figure.   The coast-line is about a thousand miles long, but it is only at the outlets of the great rivers that ports can be established. The chief are Akyab, Bassein, Rangoon, and Maulmein.   Elsewhere the coast offers only a rugged and rocky barrier to the ocean, with no available places of refuge for vessels in distress, or it is flat and muddy and unapproachable within nine or ten miles by vessels of any size ; while to the eastward, in the Tenasserim province the bare mud-banks change into an unbroken line of mangrove swamps, where the mass of fantastic roots effectually checks the inroads of the sea.

Arakan is cut off by a belt of hills from Pegu, and forms a long narrow triangle with the base to the south. The plain country is exceedingly fertile, and keeps Akyab harbour full of ships in the rice season.

Pegu, except for a few spurs from the tangled hill masses of the north and north-west, forms a vast alluvial plain, with great stretches of forest-covered hills in the north-east.

Tenasserim has also much plain-land, but with undulating ground here and there, and it is also remarkable for the fantastic outcrops of caverned limestone-rocks springing abruptly out of the plain, such as one sees in Kwangsi on the West river and in various parts of Tong-King.

The general character of the country, however, is that of a great plain intersected by a network of creeks which render it an ideal agricultural country, like Egypt, Bengal, and Mesopotamia, and rice is the thermometer of its commercial prosperity. In the north-east there are considerable tracts of hills covered with a wilderness of impenetrable forest, in which are found teak, cutch, iron-wood, and other valuable timber. This dense forest-growth in many places creeps down into the level country, and fades away through bamboo jungle into wide expanses of elephant-grass and cane. About half the area of the three provinces is cultivable, but up to now only about four thousand square miles—a tenth of the whole—are actually under cultivation. The great want of the country is population. In 1884 Mr. Bernard, the Chief Commissioner, estimated the population at a little over four millions—an increase of something like 40 per cent. in twelve years, but still a total far short of the wants of the provinces.

The progress which the province is likely to make is exemplified by the growth of the towns. Rangoon, the capital of Burma, has existed as a town for over two thousand years, but it was for long known only as the place for pilgrims to the great Shway Dagohn pagoda, the Mecca of the Indo-Chinese Buddhist to stop at. Later, it was the residence of the Regent of Pegu, as being the guard-station on the most accessible mouth of the Irrawaddy. But it was in the old days little more than a mere collection of huts. Gaspar Balbi, who visited the place three hundred years ago, mentions nothing but the monasteries, "wooden houses gilded and adorned with delicate gardens after their custom, wherein their Talapoins, which are their Friers, dwell and look to the Pagod or Varella of Dogon." In those days, and for long after, it was in Talaing hands, and it was only in 1763 that the Burmans, under Alompra, took possession of the town and gave it its present name of Rangoon. But the new name did not alter the character of the town. It remained the same collection of wattled bamboo shanties, on a marshy flat but little above the level of low tides, and intersected by narrow and irregular streets. At the beginning of the century, the town stretched along the bank for about a mile, and did not extend more than five hundred yards from the river. The official town was surrounded by a log-stockade, fortified by an indifferent kind of fosse spanned by a wooden bridge. Swine and dogs roamed at will all over the town, as they were allowed to do in Mandalay, and acted as efficient scavengers. The principal building was the Customs House, and this was just tottering into ruins, and there was a rickety erection known as the King's Wharf. Jungle grew close up to the palisading on the north, and southwards the rice-fields extended from the doors of the suburban houses right away to the mouth of the river. The town came into our hands in 1852. The morasses were filled up with earth from the higher ground inland, the stockade was pulled down, and at the present time it is impossible to realize the old dismal descriptions of the place. Now there are broad smooth roads, well laid out public gardens and parks, abundant street lamps, spacious mercantile offices, schools, mills, hospitals, gaols, law-courts, halls, and club-houses. Railways connect it with the interior; large sea-going steamers visit it in ever-increasing numbers. The population, from a paltry ten thousand, has grown to two hundred thousand, and the central town threatens soon to swallow up the neighbouring villages of Poozoondoung and Kemmendine and Kokhine, just as London has engulfed the Highgates and Kensingtons and Chelseas of last century. Rangoon claims the title of Queen of the East, and, with the new openings for trade offered by the annexation of Upper Burma, there is little doubt that she will justify the claim, and outstrip Calcutta before the end of the century. Hitherto the progress made will compare with the most vaunted of American city-successes.

Maulmein has been to some extent over-shadowed in its growth by the rapid rise of Rangoon, consequent on the transference of the government to that place. Nevertheless, we have no less cause for satisfaction in the condition of the chief town of the Tenasserim province. The Ogre's Isle, which lies in front of it, suggests the idea that the town is up a river, but, as a matter of fact, it is really on the sea-coast, with simply a large island sheltering it from the storms of the bay. It stands on the left bank of the Salween, just below its junction with the Gyaing and Attaran rivers, and is situated on the slopes of a series of low hills. Each of these surmounted by its pagoda, some glittering bright with gold-leaf orbrilliantly white in the sunlight, others crumbling away into decay and covered with moss and grass and

E

shrub-growth, while beside these are the striking outlines of the various monastic buildings, richly ornamented with carved work, gilding, and bright colour, and surrounded by masses of well-foliaged trees. Altogether the town is one of the prettiest in the East, and the view from the central ridge is certainly without its equal in Burma. The town clings to the water's edge, and is surrounded by extensive groves of every shade, from the sombre green of the mango and the mangosteen to the light tints of the pagoda-tree, interspersed with feathery clumps of bamboo and the gorgeous drooping plumes of the *Amherstia nobilis.* Beyond, green islands are set in a silvery expanse of water, their outline broken by the graceful shape of a pagoda spire, with its tinkling bells. Farther off, dark hills contrast with the silver lines of the winding rivers and the ruddy gold or tender green of the rice-fields, and away to the north rise abruptly from the plain fantastic needled peaks, honeycombed through and through with caves, most of them rendered sacred by images of the Buddha, and culminating in the rugged outcrop of the " Duke of York's Nose," a limestone ridge supposed to present the profile of that personage.

Notwithstanding the check administered by the transference of government to Rangoon, Maulmein has never ceased to grow, and has twice the population now that it had when Pegu was annexed. It is the great timber port, and, in addition, exports large quantities of rice and cotton. When trade is opened up with the Shan States, and a railway connects it with the districts to the north, it will grow still more rapidly.

The other chief ports are Akyab and Bassein. The former stands on low ground at the mouth of the Kooladan river. It has numerous public buildings, and the streets are lined with fine trees. The population numbers between 25,000 and 30,000, and large quantities of rice are exported to Europe and India; much timber, mostly iron-wood, is also sent to India for railway sleepers. Tobacco used to be raised in considerable quantities, but skill in its preparation was somewhat lamentably absent. Bassein is on what may be considered the chief mouth of the Irrawaddy, seventy-five miles from the sea. It is a neat little town of about the same population as Akyab, and clusters round about the fort which encloses the sacred Shway Moo-daw pagoda. The principal trade is in rice, for the husking of which numerous steam-mills have been erected. Other ports are Tavoy and Mergui on the Tenasserim coast, which do a yearly increasing coasting trade. The inland towns are almost exclusively on the rivers, and the chief are Pegu, formerly the Talaing capital, and noted for a very sacred pagoda; Shway Gyeen; and Toung-oo, the terminus of the Eastern Railway, shortly to be extended to Mandalay;—and on the Irrawaddy, Yandoon, a great fish-curing station; Donoobyoo; Henzadah, the centre of a very fertile district; Myan-oung, once the head-quarters of the Pegu Light Infantry, a force which demonstrated that the Burman is much too casual an individual to make a good soldier; and Prome, a place where the Buddha is said to have appeared and pro-phesied the establishment of a great empire. The Irrawaddy Valley State Railway ends here for the present, and the town has a variety of flourishing industries, notably silk cultivation. Thayetmyo was the old frontier town, and is mainly a military station, but there are petroleum-wells not far off. All of these are towns averaging something like 20,000 inhabitants, with schools and public offices. Many more might be mentioned, but enough has been said to show the character of the country; and the Burman much prefers a rural life to that of even a moderately large town.

UPPER BURMA.

The newly annexed province for the moment has greater attractions than our older divisions, though we have every reason to be proud of them and their progress. The Kachyens and the Shan hill-chiefs have during the last ten years been freeing themselves more and more from Burmese control. They have ceased to pay allegiance or tribute, and have substituted raids on the low country. It will therefore be some time before the boundaries on the eastern side are fixed; that will have to be done by arrangement with China, with whom we shall, no doubt, have to share the management of the numerous independent

hill-chieftains—a delicate matter, which nothing but just, and at the same time firm, hand-
ling will carry through successfully. It will
be enough to say that, roughly speaking, our
new province consists simply of the valley of
the Irrawaddy river, walled in by hilly table-
lands and mountain ranges (varying from
5000 feet on the east and west to 18,000 or
more on the north) on every side except the
south, where nothing but a parallel of latitude,
along which masonry pillars, from two to ten
miles distant from one another, and often
hidden in the jungle, marked the old boundary
line. The area and the character of the
country are much the same as those of Lower
Burma. There are rich alluvial plains,
intersected by barren rolling ground of no
great elevation and lines of hills, spurs from
the main ranges to east and west, joining
the watersheds between the different tributaries of the Irrawaddy. There is very
much more forest and very much less cultivation than in our sea-board provinces—the
natural results of misrule. Roads there are
practically none ; the tracks which represent
them are mere lines where the jungle has
been cut away. When a Burman makes a

wheel for his bullock-cart, he cuts it out of a solid slab of wood, leaves it square, or with imperfectly blunted corners, and trusts to time to round it for him. Even good roads would not remain long so under such traffic. No census of the country has ever been taken, and the number of our new subjects is, therefore, purely conjectural, but it probably does not exceed two millions, if indeed it reaches that figure.

This will materially reduce the already exceedingly small population per square mile of our Burma provinces, but it will bring its own remedy with it. The hostile attitude of the kings of Burma has prevented the arrival of those who would otherwise have been willing enough to settle among our subjects. This will especially be the case in Upper Burma itself. The hill-tribes have been long enough looking down enviously on the villagers settled in the fertile lowlands. In a year or so, certainly before very long, they will descend from their mountain tops and take up locations in the plain. The Shans, like the Chinamen, are born farmers and gardeners; and the Chinamen themselves —the men of Yünnan and Ssu-ch'uen—

when they see a strong and good government established in the interior, will not delay to flock after them. The Chinese are the finest race in the East, and, when they are judiciously handled, make most industrious and law-abiding subjects. The problem, therefore, is now solved. Indian immigration has been an utter failure. The Burmese detested and despised the ryots brought over, and the poor Madrassis themselves seemed incapable of doing anything. Now that the Chinamen can come on their own legs instead of having to make the long sea-voyage round by Singapore and the Straits, they will not delay to flock into the fertile lowlands of Burma, where the soil only requires to be scratched to bring forth abundant crops. Our lower provinces, as well as the new one, will profit by the disappearance of the buffer State.

THE IRRAWADDY TO MANDALAY.

There is a fairly large population in the south-eastern portion of Burma in the neighbourhood of Nin-gyan, not far from Toung-oo, but the great bulk of the people live along the banks of the Irrawaddy. Starting from the high bare slope on the right bank of the river, on which Thayetmyo is situated, one reaches the old boundary line after fourteen miles, but there is no town of any importance for about thirty more. Sin-boung-wè, where the first engagement of the war took place, is the nearest village, with no more than six or seven hundred of population. It strikingly illustrates the difference between rule and mis-rule. In the lower provinces even insignificant hamlets are neat and trim, and there is an air of order which is conspicuously absent in the squalid collection of huts inhabited by the poverty-stricken subjects of Upper Burma. Min-hla, however, was the real Burmese frontier post. Like Thayetmyo, it also stands on the right bank, and had a population of four or five thousand. The fort which was to bar the advance of our troops was on a hill on the other bank, at a bend of the river a little lower down. Kooli-gyoung was well constructed under the eye of Italian engineers, and in capable hands might have offered a prolonged resistance, but it fell to half an hour's shell-fire. The real fighting was on the other side, in the jungle round the town, between the pretty village of Ma-lohn, with its pagodas embowered in waving trees, where Sir Archibald Campbell in 1826, with a mere handful of men, routed fifteen thousand Burmese soldiery under a brother of the then king, and the town of Min-hla itself. The town was almost entirely burnt in the capture, but Min-hla is the centre of a fertile district, and is destined to become an important revenue township in the coming better days.

Ten or twelve miles above Min-hla is Ma-gway, considerably larger, and with a population of eight or nine thousand. There are some elaborate pagodas and monasteries in the neighbourhood, especially one huge gilt one on the farther bank. The town straggles a good deal, and there are a number of rude pathways lined with prickly cactus hedges, and it shows a great deal of misery, though, like the generality of Burmese towns, it is neat and cleanly kept. The constant oppression of an iniquitous government shows itself here as elsewhere. The river hereabouts is strikingly picturesque until Yay-nan-gyoung is reached. There are numerous spurs of hills crowned with the pagodas in

which the Burman so much delights; the
banks are mostly bluffs, broken with small
ravines running straight off from the river;
above the bluffs the country stretches away
in park-like uplands, with here and there
clumps of light timber, the whole very
different from the luxuriant foliage on the
banks of the river on its lower reaches in
the Pegu province.

At Yay-nan-gyoung (literally, the stream
of stinking water) the region of the earth-oil
or petroleum wells begins, and vegetation
almost entirely ceases. The town is large,
and there is a good deal of animation with
the huge, ungainly, barge-like craft used for
carrying the earth-oil. This petroleum was
one of the royal monopolies, secured by the
1867 treaty with us, and large quantities
used to be shipped to Rangoon to be manufactured into pagoda candles. But the American
rock-oil and the development of the Baku
wells interfered greatly with the sale. In
any case the workings, of which an elaborate
account may be found in Colonel Yule's
"Mission to Ava," were carried on in a very
inefficient and wasteful fashion, and the out-
put was not nearly so large or so profitable as

if Western methods had been adopted. The barren, desolate-looking stretch of country in which this earth-oil is found extends over a considerable area, but after Sin-byoo-gyoon on the right bank, with its wide sandy islands in the three-mile expanse of the river, is passed, the town of Sillay is reached. It is prettily situated on a point of high land on the eastern bank, the houses, half hidden by umbragious trees, running up the face of the slope, which has a line of fine pagodas and religious buildings along its crest. The former are encircled by some remarkable specimens of petrified wood stuck up as posts. Great quantities of petrified wood, sometimes in very large slabs, are found all along this part of the Irrawaddy. A former Governor of Sillay was particularly notorious for his anti-foreign policy. He stopped a mail-steamer and carried off the steering gear, and had an Englishman flogged. On the remonstrance of the Indian Government, he was removed from his post, to be promoted to a more important district. Sillay and Nyoung-oo, a large town twenty-eight miles farther up, are noted as the great centres of the Burmese lacquer-ware, which in its way is quite as fine as the Japanese, and only requires a few hints from Western art to become popular and command large prices in the European markets.

Nyoung-oo, however, yields in interest to the neighbouring town of Pagán, one of the ancient capitals of Burma, and now practically deserted, except for a few hundred pagoda-slaves, an outcast class condemned to lifelong and hereditary service about the religious buildings. It is practically a city of the dead, but as a religious city it is certainly the most remarkable and interesting in the world, not excepting Mecca, Kieff, or Benares. For eight miles along the river bank, and extending to a distance of two miles inland, the whole surface is thickly studded with pagodas of all sizes and shapes, and the very ground is so thickly covered with crumbling remnants of vanished shrines that, according to the popular saying, you cannot move foot or hand without touching a sacred thing. A Burmese proverb says there are 9999. This may or may not be true, but in any case it is certain that an area of sixteen square miles is practically covered with holy buildings. They are of every

order of architecture and in every stage of
decay, from the newly restored fane glittering bright in white and gold, with freshly
bejewelled "umbrella" on its spire, to the
mere tumulus of crumbling brick hardly to
be distinguished from a simple mound of
earth. Some there are with chapels and
ante-chapels, as fine as many a cathedral, and
built in the form of the Christian cross; others,
with the light 'grace of the minaret; others,
again, rounded like the Hindoo dome; some
that suggest the bamboo-modelled pagoda of
China; others, a mere Border "peel;" finally,
the ordinary bell-shaped solid mass charac-
teristic of Burma itself. The Irrawaddy
just below Pagán widens out to over two
miles, and the view of the spires and
minsters, marabouts and topes, of the
Sacred City is particularly fine and suggests
a large metropolis, a calm religious town,
perhaps, disturbed by nothing but devout
processions and gorgeous ceremonial functions, certainly anything but the solemn,
impressive solitude which is actually found.

Above Pagán the two chief towns are
Koonyua and Myin-gyan, the latter between
the two mouths of the Chin-dwin river, and
by far the most populous and busy place on

the Irrawaddy after Mandalay. It has a
population of about fifteen thousand, and,
lying as it does in the centre of a great and
fertile plain, does a trade not greatly inferior
to that of the capital itself. Considerable
quantities of rice, wheat, and cotton have
been exported in the past days, and the
amount must be greatly increased in time to
come, while the timber floated down from
the Chin-dwin forests is mostly rafted here.
Mr. Malcolm Mackenzie, who made himself
prominent in connection with the crofters'
question some time ago, had large cutch
manufactories at Myin-gyan, and there were
also some extensive cotton-mills and storing-
sheds built by King Theebaw's father.
Myin-gyan stands on the left bank, which is
here very high and abrupt, though it is
mere soil. The surrounding country is,
however, nearly quite level and open, extending in a wide plain eastward to a
huge isolated hill, believed by the Burmese to be inhabited by demons, and containing a considerable amount of iron-ore.
After Myin-gyan there are no towns of
any great importance till Mandalay, ninety
miles off, is reached. Just below the capital
the Irrawaddy contracts from a mile and

more in width to eight hundred yards, and
the stream makes a grand sweep to the west-
ward. On the left, as one ascends, are the
bare, rocky Sa-gaing hills; on the right, the
well-foliaged banks at Ava and Amarapura,
rising here and there into knolls and little
hills with rocky faces to the river front. All
three towns, Ava, Amarapura, and Sa-gaing,
if now they can be called towns, are ancient
capitals. Hence there is an abundance of
religious buildings. On the Sa-gaing hills,
stairways, some of them over a mile long,
wind up the steep slopes to the pagodas on
the top, steps in some places hewn out of the
rocky hillsides, in others laid with square
blocks of alabaster. The shrines are not
merely on the hill tops. Down on the
cramped space at the base are many more, conspicuous among them the huge solid cupola
of the " Pumpkin Pagoda." On every prac-
ticable spot of the ascent there are more,
some mere bell-shaped masses of bricks,
surmounted by the invariable "umbrella"
glittering with gold-leaf and musical with
scores of little bells, hung from the concentric
circles rising one above the other in lessening
size. Opposite, more pagodas rise up in

massive dignity on the river bank, or show their slender spires farther back against the green boughs of gigantic trees. The sight, with the background of the huge dark Shan hills to the eastward, is striking and beautiful in the extreme.

MANDALAY.

When the steamer ghaut at Mandalay is reached, the prospect is vastly different. The western hills have drawn back from the river, leaving in the foreground a wide, burnt-up sand-bank, dotted in bygone days with the relics of the royal fleet. Burmese generally have no notions of economy, and King Theebaw, even less than his father, failed to show them an example. The royal steamers, an opposition line to the Irrawaddy Flotilla Company, were driven till their machinery broke down. Then, during the rains, when this huge sand-bank was under water, they were towed over there and allowed to strand themselves and blister and rot away in the sun. There was a royal foundry, but the French engineers in charge were usually employed in laying out ornamental gardens in the Palace and endeavouring to get concessions of mines

F

for themselves. The "brasses" were all stolen
to make images of, and to set the foundry
a-going again would be little less expensive
than the original cost. On the Mandalay
side—Mandalay is on the left bank of the
Irrawaddy—there is no sand-bank, but the
view is not much more inviting. The bank
rises higher than the country behind, and it is
simply bare earth, with the royal Customs
House standing near the top, a few trees and
bamboos and ramshackle huts peeping over
the slope and a crowd of cherut-smoking loafers
collected on the bank to look at the incoming
steamer. A little higher up is the "bund,"
an embankment built to prevent the river
from flooding the town, as it used to do not
farther than ten or fifteen years back. This
embankment was declared sacred ground
when it was finished, and several Englishmen
have been put in the stocks for walking on it;
a Burman would have been flogged round
the town, or pitched into the river, if he had
been ignorant, or presumptuous, enough to
venture on such a promenade.

The capital is two miles from the river, but
there are houses and monasteries which
straggle nearly all the way down to the land-

ing-place. There is a broad, wide road running at right angles to the river, which takes
one up to a small stream called the Shway-
ta Kyoung, used to supply water for the city
moat. Along the side of this road, standing
at a little distance back from it, in the middle
of fairly large gardens of flowers and fruit
trees, are the suburban residences of some of
the Ministers. Most of these used to sleep
inside the Palace the greater part of the
year, but when they gave theatrical or other
entertainments it was in these houses outside. Perhaps it was because Ministers
and princes and great people generally in
Mandalay rode on elephants rather than in
carriages that this road was so bad. In the
wet weather it used to be a mere sea of mud ;
in dry weather it was always overhung by a
cloud of dust, like the Peking plain. A good
many large stones lay scattered about all over
it, as if there had been an idea at some time
to have it metalled, but the notion, like most
others of the kind in Mandalay, was given
up. They remained there to jolt the bones
of those who were ill-advised enough to go
up in a Mandalay bullock-carriage. These
are gay enough to look at, painted all over

in bright colours, but there are no seats. The only entrance was by a round hole in front, and you had to sit on the floor. The driver sat before you on the shafts, and prodded up the bullocks into a shambling trot. The unlucky passenger very shortly discovered that there were bones in parts of his body where previously he had imagined all was soft. Even an equipment of pillows and mattresses did not make him comfortable. In appearance they resembled nothing so much as a dog-kennel on wheels. Nevertheless, except elephants, they were the most aristocratic conveyances in the place, and the pity that was lavished on the deposed king because he had to ride down to the steamer in a "bullock-cart" was mere absurdity. To have put him on an elephant, even if it had been the Lord White Elephant, would have been cruel irony, and to have made him ride a pony would have been simply to parade his fall before the populace. His mode of departure was both the kindliest and the most honourable that could be given him.

Mandalay, like all Chinese and Indo-Chinese official towns, is divided into two—the walled city and the suburbs. The latter extend, as we have seen, two miles down to the river, and straggle for about the same distance in all directions over the level plain. The city proper is a huge walled square, each face a mile and an eighth long. The mud-mortar built walls are twenty-six feet high, machicolated at the top; they are three feet thick, backed with a heavy mass of earth, and along the ramparts are wooden look-out towers of an ornate style of architecture suggestive of China. There are twelve gates to the city, three on each side, but only one bridge over the moat to each three, except on the west, where there are two. The moat is about sixty feet from the walls, and considerably more than that wide, covered in many places with the lotos-plant that the Buddhist loves. Here and there upon it float royal craft, state barges, and despatch-boats, gilt from stem to stern, and manned by sometimes as many as sixty paddlers. The city is well and regularly laid out. From the gates roughly macadamized roads, a hundred feet wide, run parallel to the walls. They are lined with young trees (Mandalay only exists since 1857), and down the sides of most of them run little streams of water. Between these main streets, and parallel to them, are others narrower, but still very orderly. There is no attempt at a drainage system, but the town is essentially clean and airy, thanks to the unmolested, or rather cherished, pigs and dogs that act as highly efficient scavengers, and the constant open spaces insuring ventilation. Forming a species of redoubt in the centre of the city is the Palace, which has two successive enclosures—the outer, a log stockade, with elaborate turreted gateways; the inner, a brick wall; with a broad esplanade between the two. In the exact centre of the Palace and of the city rises the seven-roofed spire, emblematic of royalty and religion, which the Burmese look upon as the centre of Burma and therefore of creation. Apart from the Supreme Court and Hall of Audience, the royal dwelling consists mainly of a rambling succession of gardens and pleasure or residential houses. The higher officials live within the Palace stockade, and there also are the mint, arsenal, treasury, powder-magazines, and other public buildings.

In the walled city live the lower officials and the soldiery, and, in the suburbs outside, the traders and general population. This is estimated all round at something over a hundred thousand. There is a good deal of wealth in the commercial town, but it is in the hands of Chinese and Moguls, with whom the king was afraid to meddle. No Burman could get rich with safety.

Scattered about over the outer town are great numbers of pagodas and monasteries and religious buildings. The monastic population is especially great. It has been estimated as high as thirty thousand. Chief of the monasteries is the king's. This royal monastery is a mass of gilding from the roof to the side-posts, inside and out. The eaves and the top of the side walls are covered with the bold, open carving in which the Burmese show so much artistic skill, and this is as richly gilt as everything else. The boxes in which the palm-leaf manuscripts are kept are as elaborate in decoration as the commentaries themselves are valuable to students of Buddhist literature. Among the pagodas the most interesting is the so-called " Incomparable Pagoda." Round about the main shrine, which in itself is a marvel of decoration, there are many rows of other smaller ones, each sheltering a series of marble slabs in shape and appearance not unlike large gravestones. On these are engraved the *Tripitaka*, the "three baskets of the Law," the Buddhist scriptures. The uncle of King Theebaw, known as the War Prince, was a very pious man notwithstanding the desire to fight the English which gained him his name. In order to lay up good store of "merit" towards a future existence, he called together the most learned monks of his time to settle the best authenticated version of the holy books, and this authorized and revised edition he had deeply engraved on these marble slabs, so that it might endure to all time and gain him a seat in the blissful dwellings of Brahmas. The idea may or may not have been borrowed from the similar work executed in China, but at any rate the Atooma-shee pagoda will be of great interest to Pali scholars throughout the world. But this is only one of many fanes, some marvellous for their size, some for their beauty, some for the multitude of offerings made to them.

The streets are a curious study. There is an extraordinary variety of nationalities to be seen constantly in Mandalay. Every here and there one comes across a band of Shans, tall, stalwart men, very Chinese in feature, wearing usually nothing but baggy blue trousers, and tattooed from the waist down to the ankles. Occasionally, too, though much more rarely of late years, one comes across a Kachyen hill-chieftain with his train of ragged followers, slight, but wiry, in figure, with aquiline noses and shifty, fierce eyes, as different as possible from the thickset, open-faced Burman. Then there are parties of Arakanese, come over the hills to worship at the most holy " Arakan Pagoda," with its famous brass Gautama, said to have been cast from a model of the great Master himself, and to have been inspired with life by him for a day in response to ardent prayers. The Arakanese are easily recognized by the modification of their Mongolian features induced by their neighbourhood to the Bengalis. They have more of a nose and more hair on the face, and altogether greater regularity of feature. Moreover, their rolling *r*'s betray them. The Burman, like the Chinaman, has

not an *r* in his alphabet. Besides these, there
are Chins from the western hills : the men
with their hair gathered up in a knot over
the forehead, and very often not much more
clothing than a small-sized handkerchief; the
women, with their faces tattooed all over with
close dark-blue lines to prevent non-Chin
lovers from running away with them, dressed
in short smocks and still shorter waistcloths,
which display sturdy legs exceedingly freely.
Along with them may be seen a Chaw or two,
the men with their foreheads shaved liked a
Madrasi, the women with their hair plaited in
two tails and brought up round the forehead
like a coronal ; sun-and-moon worshipping
Shandoos ; Karenns in long blouses marked
with lines and embroidery according to the
tribe they belong to ; Khamis and Mros from
the northern Arakan hill-tracts, whose scanty
beards and oblique eyes remind one of the
Annamese ; and the Paloung come down from
the north with his bamboo rafts laden with
pickled tea. It is a great place, Mandalay, for
the study of queer tribes and primitive superstitions. Under native rule it used to be the
refuge of the sweepings of all the country,
British and independent. Alongside the

holy, yellow-robed, shaven-headed monks
might be seen gamblers, thieves, broken
agriculturists, and military bullies and hangers-
on of the great men about the Court, not a few
of them Europeans, runaways from ships in
Rangoon harbour and from justice, ready to
do anything but honest work, some of them
advising the king in his foreign relations and
acting as generals in his army, others simply
living on the families of their Burmese wives.
Then there were honest traders, Chinese and
Moguls, indifferent honest perhaps, but at
any rate substantial : the Chinaman smooth-
shaven and prosperous, whether big and raw-
boned from Yünnan and Ssu-ch'uen, or thickset
and plump from Rangoon and the Straits—
Baba Babas, "eleven o'clock Chinamen," as
they are called—born and brought up in
British territory and without a notion of what
the Flowery Land and its mandarin system is
like; the Mogul with his red-dyed beard,
solemn face, and his cunning, that of a Jew —
plus an Armenian plus a Greek, and yet only
just able to hold his own with the Chinaman,
who has his gorgeous joss-house in the out-
skirts of Mandalay with the proud inscription,
" Enlightenment finds its way even among the

outer barbarians." It was a town of very violent contrasts, Mandalay—the silk-clad Chinaman elbowing the ninety-nine hundredths naked Chin ; the mendicant of the Sacred Order of the Yellow Robe looking pityingly on the grim-visaged Mogul, who could buy up half the town ; the haughty Minister preceded by the shrieking mandarin, his lictor ; the cashiered French officer hobnobbing with a favourite spittoon-bearer ; gilded temples and jewelled monasteries by the side of trumpery bamboo shanties that one could knock over with a sweep of the leg ; lottery offices next door to substantial traders ; the royal cotton-mills standing in the midst of a nest of professional fortune-tellers ; and over every one the fear of denunciation to the Court, of the prison and the rack, or the crucifix. In a year or two more it will be one of the most popular garrison stations in Burma and the haunt of the globe-trotter.

THE IRRAWADDY ABOVE MANDALAY.

The river scenery between Mandalay and Bhamô (or Bamaw, as it is pronounced) is the finest in Burma, and is all the more pleasurable because one gradually gets rid of the eternal pagodas which make the whole extent of the lower river look not unlike a big graveyard. An hour's steaming from Mandalay brings you to the Mingohn pagoda, a huge mass of bricks four hundred feet square at the base, and intended to rise to a height of five hundred feet. It was, however, never finished, and an earthquake in 1839 rent the gigantic cube with fantastic fissures from top to bottom. A queer cavernous slit enables you, if you can hold on tight, to scramble up to the top, whence a grand view may be had of the wide silvery Irrawaddy, the gilded spires of Mandalay, and the pagoda-sprinkled heights of Sa-gaing. There is a curious chimney-stack like erection rising some twenty feet above the level of the summit, and extending, it is said, all the way to the base, the object of which is not apparent. Close to the great pagoda hangs the largest bell in Burma, second only in size to the monster at Moscow. It is eighteen feet high, seventeen from lip to lip, and eighteen inches in thickness. The weight is over ninety tons, and has proved too much for the supports, for one side of the bell rests on the ground. All around are gigantic mango and tamarind trees.

Above this the river banks become more and more deserted. Here and there is a small fishing village, looking even more dismal and dilapidated than those below the royal city. The larger towns, such as Malay, Sheen-pagah, Katha, and Shway-goo, are simply places where a few thousand people gather together and keep from starving. Beyond these is the Third Defile, where the stream narrows to a thousand yards, and flows for thirty miles through a low undulating tangle of hills, covered with luxuriant forest-growth, noble palmyras, and gigantic clumps of bamboos, relieved by the pale tropical green of the tamarind and the plantain growing close down to the water's edge and trailing great creepers into the stream itself. It is almost like lake scenery, each long reach of deep smooth water seeming barred by wooded cliffs. Huge fresh-water dolphin tumble their round heads about in the stream, or race with the steamer, while overhead snowy egrets and gay paroquets fly past the occasional heavy flapping hornbill, and flocks of monkeys on the banks chatter defiance at the noisy paddle-steamer. Half way through the defile is a small rocky island with a pagoda and monastery on it. The monks here, as in many other places in Burma, have so tamed the fish that they will come to their call and will feed out of the hand.

Beyond this defile there is flat country again, with the lofty Kachyen and Shan hills looming in the distance. Here again are a few villages, whose inhabitants live in constant fear of raids from the wild hill-tribes and visits from scarcely more fierce tigers. Tagoung and Old Pagán, ancient capitals, are passed, and then the Second Defile is reached —a magnificent gorge which is one of the sights of the country. The river, above and below quite a mile wide, here narrows to three hundred yards, to burst at right angles through the mountain range. For five miles one winds round gigantic precipices, covered with stunted trees, while here and there a bald peak rises like a vulture's head from among the forest-growth, festooned clumps of palms, bamboos, and graceful musæ alternating with the broad-leafed eng-tree and the mast-like oil-palm. In the middle of the defile stands the Deva-faced cliff, the Angel

Rock, as it is called—a wall of stone rising six
hundred or more feet sheer out of the water,
the trees on the summit looking like so much
heather.   In the rains several rivulets leap
over the side, breaking into spray before they
are a quarter of the way down.   Perched on
a great boulder at the base is the little
Sessoungan pagoda, where sure-footed wor-
shippers deposit offerings to be eaten by the
long-tailed monkeys that abound in the defile.
There is a wonderful echo in the gorge: a
gun discharged reverberates like a park of
artillery; the call of the water-bird floats
weirdly from cliff to cliff, and sinks away in
the distance; the hum of the bees on the
flowering shrubs booms from side to side like
the notes of a great organ ; and the splash of
the paddle-wheels raises a continuous roar
like that of Niagara.   Bottom has not been
found at sixty fathoms.   At each short turn
the river seems to rise bodily out of the
mountains.   Suddenly we turn round a peak
with great lanes torn through the forest-
growth on its sides by descending boulders,
and we are in the level country again, with a
great plain before us extending to the foot of
the Kachyen hills, and half way up which,
twenty miles off, lies Bhamô.

Bhamô is the navigation limit for steamers on the Irrawaddy, and there used to be deep water immediately under the high bank on which the town stands. The channels, however, seem to have changed recently. The Irrawaddy here, nevertheless, eight hundred miles and more from the sea, is three-quarters of a mile wide, so that there can be no difficulty in keeping open the river communication. The town of Bhamô practically consists of a single street a mile and a quarter long, following closely the bank of the river. On the land face there is a log stockade ten feet high, about four hundred yards from the river-side, and intended to keep out reiving hill-men and prowling tigers. The population is about 2500, and is mostly Shan-Burmese, a cross between the old inhabitants and the hill-men of the adjoining principality of Momeit. Perhaps a quarter of the inhabitants are Chinamen, and they are certainly the most important people there. They have the best houses and all the money, but very few of them are permanent residents. They come over with a caravan, transact their business and make their purchases, and then return over to Yung-chang or Tali, leaving perhaps

G

a clerk or two to make investments against their return and to see about the disposal of what goods may remain over.

The idea that China would ever take, or even wanted, Bhamô never entered any one's brain three or four years ago. The place was certainly captured and held for some months in the beginning of 1885 by a combined band of Chinese and Kachyens, but the Chinamen were just as much robbers as the Kachyens were, and their action was disavowed by the Imperial Government as well as by the provincial Governor-General. Between Bhamô and the foot of the hills to the east extends a plain about twelve miles wide, all cultivable land, but at present covered with bamboo and other jungle, with stretches of elephant-grass. The Kachyen hills then interpose a strip of neutral territory, some twenty or twenty-five miles wide, between Burma and China, and the peoples then reached are Chinese Shans rather than Chinamen. We have therefore on this side as satisfactory a frontier as could be desired— a thing which it would have been impossible to obtain if the Middle Kingdom had crossed the watershed. The railway to be constructed from Toung-oo to Mandalay will be pushed on through an easy country to Bhamô, and then we shall have a junction with the Indian railway system at Dibrogurh in sight.

Some score miles or so above Bhamô the Irrawaddy passes through the First Defile. This is as grand as the Second, but infinitely wilder. The river is narrowed from a thousand yards to a hundred and fifty, and rushes through sheer walls of rock. Prodigious boulders in mid-stream produce eddies and backwaters and whirlpools, and render all navigation impossible except for the smallest boats, and even for these it is a very dangerous matter. These narrow gullets, one of them no more than fifty yards wide, are repeated several times, with quiet but rapid reaches in between, until the " Elephant and Cow" are reached. After these two fantastic rocks are passed, the stream widens out again, and, after receiving the Tapeng river from the eastern hills, flows on quietly to Bhamô. The sources of the Irrawaddy have never been seen, but it is now definitely settled that the Sanpu, the mysterious river of Tibet, is not the upper Irrawaddy, as has

G 2

long been asserted. The Sanpu is undoubtedly the Dihong. Above the junction
with the Mogoung river, the Irrawaddy splits
into two, the Myit-gyee and Myit-ngè (the
large and small river), and at this point is
nine hundred yards across. It seems therefore probable that the source of one or other
of the arms must be a lake to produce this
huge volume of water. In any case the
Irrawaddy is one of the finest rivers in the
world—certainly one of the finest navigable
rivers.

III.—THE PEOPLE.

BURMESE KINGS.

FROM the brief glance we had of the history of Burma, especially of the connections we have had with the Burmese, it might be supposed that they are an entirely objectionable race. Nothing could be more unjust with regard to the people at large. Their rulers have been bad enough, and indeed a Burman in authority, even under our control in the lower provinces, is not always the most amiable of personages. To mention a Burmese policeman to an Anglo-Burman, or even to a Burman for the matter of that, has much the same effect as squirting hot water into his ear. He becomes voluble and abusive on the spot. Conceit is the greatest fault of the Burman. In some respects it is not altogether a bad quality, but it entirely depends upon your point of view with regard to the person who exhibits it. The Burmese kings exhibited it in most grandiose fashion. The first Burmese War was described in the following fashion :—·

"The white strangers from the West fastened a quarrel upon the Lord of the Golden Palace. They landed at Rangoon, took that place and Prome; and were permitted to advance as far as Yandabo; for the king, from motives of piety and regard to life, made no effort whatever to oppose them. The strangers·had spent vast sums of money on the enterprise; and by the time they reached Yandabo their resources were exhausted, and they were in great distress. They petitioned the king, who, in his clemency and generosity, sent them large sums of money to pay their expenses back, and ordered them out of the country."

The strangers, however, have stayed ever since in the provinces of Arakan and Tenasserim, and they were rude enough to call the money for their expenses an indemnity. Shortly before the above declaration, the king had sent a note to Sir Archibald Campbell representing that " it was contrary to his religious principles and the constitution of the empire to make any cession of territory, and he was bound to preserve its integrity." The king was referred to as the "emperor of emperors, against whose imperial majesty if any shall be so foolish as to imagine anything, it shall be happy for them to die and be consumed ; the Lord of great charity and help of all nations ; the Lord esteemed for happiness ; the Lord of all riches, of elephants and horses, and all good blessings ; the Lord of high-built palaces of gold ; the great and most powerful Emperor in this life, the soles of whose feet are gilt and set upon the heads of all people."

The Burmese " Royal Chronicle of Kings " enumerates 587,000 and some odd hundreds of these distinguished personages. Age did not stale their infinite variety, but, on the whole, it is a matter of congratulation that the world has done with them. The founder of the dynasty of which King Theebaw was the last representative was a very favourable specimen. Aloung Payah stood five feet eleven inches, a great height for a Burman, and was of a very athletic build. He was fighting all his life, and therefore had no time for the simple massacres which his descendants indulged in. But he had a right royal opinion of himself. A Captain Baker, the commander of an East Indiaman, was sent by the Company to enter into relations with him. He brought the king a present of a few chests of gunpowder, a couple of muskets, a gilt looking-glass, some lavender-water, and some red earth in bags, and offered him the assistance of the Company. The captain evidently looked upon Aloung Payah as little better than a savage, and was somewhat astonished at the king's defiant laughter and the self-confidence of his reply :—

"Have I asked or do I want any assistance to reduce my enemies to subjection ? Let none conceive such an opinion! Have I not in three years' time extended my conquests three months' journey in every quarter without the help of cannons or muskets ? Nay, I have, with bludgeons only, opposed and defeated these Peguans who destroyed the capital of this kingdom, and took the prince prisoner; and a month hence I intend to go with a great force to Dagohn [Rangoon,] when I will advance to the walls of Pegu, blockade and starve them out of it, which is the last town I have now to take to complete my conquest, and then I will go in quest of Bournon [the French governor of Syriam, whom he afterwards did put to death]. Captain, see this sword; it is now three years since it has been constantly exercised in chastising my enemies; it is indeed almost blunt with use; but it shall be continued to the same till they are utterly dispersed. Do not talk of assistance. I require none. The Peguans I can wipe away as thus [drawing the palm of one hand over the other]. See these arms and this thigh [drawing his loose coat-sleeves up to the arm-pit, and lifting his waist-cloth so as to display a brawny tattooed leg]; amongst a thousand you cannot see my match. I can crush a hundred such as the King of Pegu."

He also announced that he intended seeking the French out in Madras, and that if a nine-pounder shot were to hit him it could do him no harm, with a good deal more to the same effect. But he at any rate was a great commander. His successors had all his arrogance without his abilities.

One of them goes by the name of the drunkard, or fisherman king, both pastimes, fishing as well as drinking, being abhorred by good Buddhists. Another announced that he was the fifth Buddha who is to appear in this world cycle. The monks refused to believe it, so he cut the heads off a few thousand of them and commenced building the Mingohn pagoda, not far from Mandalay, which, even in its present unfinished state, is the largest mass of brickwork in the world. After him several of the line were subject to fits of insanity, but even in their madness they did not commit such atrocities as when they thought the matter calmly out. Tharrawaddy had a celestial spear which he always kept by him, and occasionally used to spit a courtier, and it was in his time that the idea sprang up that the ordinary amusement of kings of Burma was to sit at their parlour window and shoot their subjects as they passed by. His son, Moung Lohn, the " old king " as he is called in Burma, King Theebaw's father, was much the best king the country ever had. He was very pious, did many good works, and was particularly fond of his title " Convenor of

the fifth great synod," but even in his time
there were sudden deaths, even of his own
sons. The king would say emphatically,
" I don't want to see that man any more,"
and he did not. The offender died of
" official colic " within a few hours.

Of King Theebaw very little need be said.
He was a weak creature, entirely under the
control of his harridan queen and her mother.
The latter was described the other day as
" the ordinary type of old woman." Happily
this is a libel. Ordinary old women, even in
Burma, do not have their step-sons and
daughters and their coadjutor or sister wives
killed by the half-dozen. That was the point
about King Theebaw that his subjects did
not like. They did not mind the massacreings; that was quite proper, and sanctioned by
old custom ; but that he should have only one
wife seemed to them undignified and weakly
in the extreme. By the actual Constitution
of the country he ought to have had four—
the queens of the north, south, east, and west
palaces—and as many more " inferior " wives
as he cared for. The pious and enlightened
monarch, his father, had fifty-three recognized
wives, besides an indefinite number of hand-

maidens. By the wives he had one hundred and ten children, forty-eight sons and sixty-two daughters. The children of the hand-maidens were not counted, partly because they were not worth killing in the event of a disputed succession. Careful statisticians aver that the orthodox old gentleman averaged seven children a year. Against this record Theebaw could only show five children in five years, and three of these were dead. Such an unkingly state of things seemed to the Burmese people in the highest degree indecorous.

BURMESE OFFICIALS.

With kings of the character we have seen, it is not to be wondered at that the Ministers and officials of lower rank were not very estimable people. This was not because there was no system of administration. On the contrary, the governmental institutions were ancient, well developed, and elaborate down to the minutest details. The number, rank, and functions of the Ministers were strictly defined by precedent, and they were supposed to be appointed for special abilities.

There is no hereditary rank, out of the royal blood, in Burma any more than there is in China or in any of the Indo-Chinese countries. Any one might become a Minister, and, indeed, instances in which men of the lowest rank, and even coolies, have risen to the highest posts have been far from uncommon. But it was much easier to fall than to rise, and, as every one's position depended upon the king, the country suffered just as much as if no Constitution existed at all. Therefore a Burmese Minister never did anything but take the utmost care that he was neither beheaded nor tortured nor dismissed. All that he ever accomplished in the way of forming a policy was to suggest that the Lord of the Golden Throne might like such and such a thing done. But even so much as that was only ventured upon by extremely conscientious men or by personal favourites. As for the ordinary run of officials, when they were questioned about their departments, they gathered, or guessed, from the questions, what was expected to be done, and then declared that it was done, and afterwards proceeded to do it.

Nevertheless, the number, rank, and functions

of the different officers were strictly defined by precedent. The absolute power of the king, the despotic character of the government when a weak, vicious, or ignorant man was at the head of it, rendered the working of the Constitution a mere farce. The country suffered just as much as if there were absolute chaos. Still, a sketch of the administrative system may be interesting.

There were two classes of Burmese Ministers:

1. The *Woon-gyees*, who were the administrative officers properly so called; and

2. The *A-twin-woons*, whose authority and responsiblity were confined to the Palace.

On paper, their duties and position were quite distinct, but, as a matter of fact, as long as we have any knowledge of the conduct of Burmese affairs, the officers of the household have had quite as much to do with the affairs of the nation as the class to whom these were supposed especially to belong. Every one was prepared, and was very often called upon, to do everything—to advise on matters of state, politics, finance, or revenue; to try a case, civil or criminal; direct military or naval operations (from an elephant on the river bank), or superintend the building of a royal pagoda or other work of merit. One of the officers of the household was, in fact, appointed commander-in-chief, under King Theebaw, of the army which made so slight a resistance in the third Burmese War. He knew nothing about military weapons or military tactics, but that was a matter which did not greatly concern either him or the king.

Technically, there were only four *Woongyees* and four *A-twin-woons*, but this number was not unseldom exceeded. The *Woon-gyees* were naturally the more important officers, and they, with the lower grades of the same department, constituted the Great Council of State, the *Hloht-daw*, or *Hloot-daw* as it is sometimes written.

THE HLOHT-DAW.

As this Council has been retained, probably only as a temporary measure, since the occupation of the country, a detailed description of it may be of some interest. The *Hloht* was Cabinet, House of Legislature, and Supreme Court of Justice rolled in one, and there was no appeal from its decisions, unless the king changed his mind. It was this Council that summarily decided the case of the Bombay Burma Trading Corporation which was the immediate cause of the ultimatum despatched to King Theebaw. It used to meet in a building situated between the royal eastern gate of the Palace and the outer gate of the Palace enclosure, on the wide esplanade or court-yard. Each Minister had his special office at no great distance on this same esplanade. If rule were observed, the king himself, or, failing him, the heir apparent or some one of the royal blood, was the president. But King Theebaw issued all his orders beforehand, and the *Hloht* only assembled to hear them announced by the Taing-dah Woon, who was his great favourite and adviser. If there could be said to be a president, it was the Kin-woon *Min-gyee*, the so-called Prime Minister, the one able and experienced man in the Council as it existed under King Theebaw. He was in England in 1872, and ever since then represented order and the peace party in Mandalay. But he was no favourite of the king's, and would probably have been made away with long ago had it not been that he held a patent, given him under the seal of King Mindohn, guaranteeing him from being put to death by any of an extraordinarily lengthy and categorically set forth list of methods of execution. Inventive genius was often sorely tried in endeavouring to find out a process against which he was not safeguarded.

The Ministers who composed the Hloht were not divided by any sharply defined line as superior and ministerial, though the titles assigned to them seemed to point to some such distinction of grades. Nominally, there were fourteen grades, and eleven of these properly consisted of four members, each ranking by seniority. Power, or the want of it, however, entirely depended upon the freaks of the king. Colonel Sladen no doubt has arranged some system of precedency if it was considered worth while, for the Council cannot last long.

The *Woon-gyees* or *Min-gyees* were the first in rank. *Woon* means "burden"— metaphorically, the burden of State affairs; actually, a burden to the people. The usual rendering in English was Secretary of State, and, if the title was to be translated at all, this was undoubtedly the best rendering. As

H

said above, each of these Ministers had his own department or departments, but the distribution of work was an entirely personal matter, and was never definitely fixed. Indeed, though the *Woon-gyees*, like the king himself, had always territorial as well as a host of other titles, even these were not attached to the office, but were given from time to time by the man who arranged everything, the king. As in the rest of Indo-China and in China itself, these titles were not hereditary.

Next to the *Woon-gyees* ranked two officers, the *Myin-thoo-gyee Woon*, or Master of the Horse, the commander of the chief cavalry regiment and representative of the mounted services generally, and the *Athee Woon*, who had charge of the concerns of all people not in the royal service. His duties were a mere sinecure, for no one would have had the slightest chance of getting the better of a dispute with any one in the royal employment. Neither of these officers had much to do in the Council, unless they were told off for some special service not included in their departmental scheme.

Following these came the *Woon-dauks*. *Dauk* means a "prop." The *Woon-dauks* were therefore assistants of the *Woon-gyees*, and may be called Assistant Secretaries of State. They also were properly four in number, but there were usually many more. The rank was often conferred for a special purpose, as when an envoy was sent abroad, or sometimes as a reward for good service. Each *Woon-dauk* had a department, or perhaps several, assigned to him, but he no more confined himself to the duties of that department, or necessarily performed any one of them, than any other Burmese official. As a general rule, however, all matters that were not important enough, or too troublesome, for the *Woon-gyees* were left in their hands. These two classes practically did all the work there was to do, and formed the real Ministry.

Below the *Woon-dauks* came four officials called *Ná-kan-daws*, "receivers of the royal ear." They formed a species of Black Rod, and carried messages from the king to the Council and from the Council to the king. The royal words were too precious and weighty to be borne by word of mouth, and therefore these officials wrote them down in large note-books in gorgeously gilded covers, and carried these in both hands ostentatiously before them, as insignia of their office and intimation that nothing was to bar their way.

The fifth grade was that of the *Sayay-daw-gyees,* "the great royal writers." They had much more important duties than those of mere secretaries, and, as the great bulk of the administrative work fell on them, the technical number of four was always greatly exceeded, and there were seldom fewer than a score. They were, in fact, executive officers, and may be compared to the registrar of a court, with a good deal more multifarious work than falls to the lot of that functionary. To them fell the task of holding preliminary investigations in important judicial matters, and sometimes they would even decide minor cases themselves, subject to the approval of one of the superior Ministers. All matters of detail were left to them, and, as an immediate consequence, no *Woon* could do anything without his *Sayay-daw-gyee.*

Allied to them, but with considerably inferior powers, though not less work, were the *Ame-n-daw-yays,* the "writers of royal orders." The name is not inaptly chosen, for the decrees were as much personal edicts as any *ukase* or *hatti humayoum*, and the Government occupied a mere formal position in the orders, which related to the appointment and transfer of officers, the collection of revenue, raising and marching of troops, leases of forests, and hundreds of other matters.

Ranking below them were the *A-thohn-sayays*, "the work writers," whose duties were very much those of the members of a public works department. They were supposed to keep roads and bridges in order, to repair public buildings, and build new ones when they were required. Except in their latter capacity, and in clearing the city streets for a royal progress, their duties were very perfunctorily performed.

The eighth grade is that of the *A-hmat-sayays*, the "notice writers." They drafted and wrote out all orders, injunctions, and letters issued or to be issued by the Council.

Allied to them in duties were the *A-way-youk-sayays*, the "clerks for matters from afar." They received, read, made a *précis* of, and docketed all letters sent from a distance, whether from a remote province or from some independent country. With the last grade, in fact, they were the correspondence clerks, and did all the more laborious and irksome work of the *Woons*. They had naturally large numbers of assistants in training for these and higher posts.

The tenth grade was that of the *Than-daw-kans*, the "receivers of the royal voice." These were merely ceremonial officers, and there were only two of them. It was the custom in Burma to hold periodical *Kadaw-pwès*; "beg-pardon days" they were usually called. On such occasions, all officials, and chieftains who held their principalities under the king, were expected to come and do homage in the great Hall of Audience. There were usually three such functions in the year, but sometimes there were more. New Year's Day, which in Burma falls in April, and the end of the Buddhist Lent, in October, were invariable dates. The duty of the *Than-daw-kans* was to make lists of those who had attended, to read the letters of those who had sent excuses, and to report the names of defaulters. In former days it was a favourite trick of Burmese kings to receive our representatives on such "beg-pardon days," so that it might appear to the people that he was recognized as suzerain over all foreign nations. It may be remarked that when Chinese envoys came they were always present at such receptions, a fact which may be fairly set against the vapourings of the *Peking Gazette.*

Of the same character were the *Letsoung-sayays,* the "present clerks." No one could go before the king without making a present. The gift or gifts were announced aloud by these officials before the throne. They correspond to the *Tosha-khana* clerks of India.

The *Yohn - zaw* was a kind of Master of Ceremonies. He superintended all the arrangements for audiences, notified the officials who were expected to attend, and informed them what business was to be transacted, what dresses they were to wear, and such-like details.

Under him was the *Necha,* or usher, who pointed out to each official, or visitor, the place he was to occupy at ceremonial meetings of the Council and at levées. The places in the *Hloht-daw* are marked by little holes in the floor—a circumstance which has a rather curious origin. The floor is raised off the ground on piles, and, underneath, each man had his servant with his pipe. The attendant thrust up the long stem through the hole in the planking and held the bowl below. In later days the pipes have been mostly given up, but the holes remain. Smoking is so universal in Burma that it was not considered at all out of place for the highest Minister to hold a cigar in his hand while he made his reverence to the king, and his Majesty himself puffed away vigorously all the time.

The lowest in rank of the officials of the *Hloht* were the *Thissa - daw - sayays*, the "royal oath clerks." It was their business to administer the oath of fealty to all who entered the king's service. The ceremony is somewhat curious, and was based on an old legend, which obtains currency in Siam as well as in Burma, and results in similar formalities. The oath was written down on paper as follows :—

"I, the most glorious and famous Lord of the Celestial Elephant, and Lord of many White Elephants, Lord of the Heavenly Weapon, and Sovereign of the whole world, declare that if you [here was inserted the candidate's name] obey and follow my commands, you will be free from all the ninety-six diseases and from the eight accidents, under the aid of the five thousand *Nats* [spirits] that guard religion, the *Nats* that guard the trees, the *Nats* that guard the earth, the *Nats* that guard the skies, and all kinds of *Nats*, the *Nats* that guard the forest, the *Nats* that guard the hills, the *Nats* that guard the five great rivers, the *Nats* that guard the five hundred little rivers, the *Nats* that guard the Irrawaddy, the Thawlawaddy, the Dohttawaddy, all the *Nats* that guard the rivers, and the *Nats* that guard the Pohppa hill; but if you break your oath which you have ratified by drinking this water, in which swords and spears have been dipped, then may you die by these weapons."

This was read over in a temple before an image of the Buddha, the candidate for office repeating the words after the *Thissa-daw-sayay*. Then the paper was burnt and the ashes were stirred up in a cup full of water, with a little bundle of models of the five kinds of weapons used by the Burmese, the bow the spear, the sword, the rifle, and the cannon. The person to be sworn in drank this, ashes and all, and could be called upon to repeat this formality of "the water of the oath" at pleasure. All foreigners who entered the king's service had to go through this ceremony.

This completes the list of the officers of the *Hloht-daw*, the Supreme Council of State.

THE OFFICERS OF THE HOUSEHOLD.

The chamber, or place of assembly, of the officials charged with the duties of the interior of the Palace was called the *Byè-deht*. *Byè* is said to be a Talaing word meaning "bachelor," so that the place would bear the name of the bachelors' room. Formerly, it is said, the king's pages in waiting used the *Byè-deht* as an ante-chamber, and the king himself is said to have come occasionally to see his elephants exercised there. Of late years, however, the chamber has been exclusively used as a public office. It might be called the Court of Privy Council.

Of this second order of Ministers, the *A-twin-woons*, "interior Ministers," were the highest in rank. Their principal business was supposed to be the conveying of important matters of discussion from the *Hloht-daw* to the king, but they actually concerned themselves with everything or nothing, according to the degree of favour in which they stood. They slept in turn, two at a time, in the Palace, as indeed almost all the officers of the Council did. The *A-twin-woons* ranked above the *Woon-dauks*.

There were four other grades in this class, but, except the second in rank, the others were of little importance. These were the *Than-daw-zins*, the "royal voice trans-mitters." They were always in close attend-ance at levées, and on other occasions took down the king's orders and carried them to whomsoever they might concern. They also bore forth in state, royal letters from the Palace, and were therefore attached to all missions.

The others, the *Byè-deht Than-zin*, the *See-mee-htoon-hmoo*, and the *Tin-dan-tan-hmoo*, were no doubt officials, and thought a good deal of themselves, but their duties were rather those of a menial than of a Privy Councillor. They kept a record of every one sleeping within the Palace stockade, and warned those required when it was their turn to remain all night, looked after the lighting of the royal buildings, the furniture and appointments, and the like. Any one found inside the main gate after dark whose name was not down in their books would have been liable to grave suspicion and consequent punishment. These officers had, therefore, not a little power in their hands, and were practically a species of secret police.

METHOD OF APPOINTMENT AND PAYMENT.

There was no system of literary examination in Burma, as there is in nearly all the other Indo-Chinese countries, for appointment to office. Rise to office depended upon chance or favour. Several of King Theebaw's most trusted advisers have been his body-slaves.

This was not a very satisfactory way of administering the country, and the way in which the officials drew their pay was still less so. Each officer had given to him a province, district, or town to govern for the king's and his own benefit. From this appointment he got his territorial title and his living. He was *Myo-sah*, or "town-eater," of such and such a place. Most of these devourers of the people were non-resident, and had to appoint deputies, and these deputies also drew their salaries by fleecing the people. The division of the country for the collection of the revenue was identical with that for administrative purposes, and the several duties were carried on by the same persons with the same assistants. The one man was civil administrator, judge, colonel of the local militia, and revenue collector for his locality, whether province, circle, or simple village. The fixed revenue demanded by the *Myo-sah*, whether prince of the blood royal, Minister, maid of honour, royal spittoon-bearer, coxswain of a despatch boat, or Lord White Elephant, was remitted to Mandalay by the deputy-lieutenant of the province, together with a certain overplus for the *Myo-sah's* secretary, clerk, and treasurer. The more a man cultivated, the more grievously was he squeezed, so that all enterprise and industry were long ago crushed out of the life of the Upper Burman. Wheat grows in abundance wherever it is planted, but hardly any one dared to cultivate it lest he should be called upon to pay double rates. It was the same with cotton, sugar-cane, Indian corn, and sessamum. Upper Burma might have grown quantities of tea, tobacco, indigo, and cutch, but the terrible system of government drove all life out of the people, and only showed danger in what ought to have been a profit. Teak was a royal monopoly, but there were other valuable woods everywhere throughout the forests, yet no one dared cut them, even to build himself a house, lest a comfortable house should suggest hidden riches.

THE PEOPLE.

It is not at all wonderful, therefore, that the natives of the country we have just annexed were somewhat soured in their disposition. Years of grinding oppression changed courage into something like ferocity, and open-heartedness into gloom and sus-picion. Nevertheless, the rapidity with which one of King Theebaw's subjects assimi-lated his ways to those of our seaboard provinces showed that nothing was wanted but changed conditions of life to make a light-hearted creature of him. It was not easy for him to cross the frontier, for all the outlets were well guarded, and the relations of any man who was known to have settled in the lower provinces were put to death; but the number that steadily every year came to establish themselves in Pegu was quite sufficient to show that the settlement of our new possession will be neither a long nor a troublesome matter. The arrival of our troops in the country was marked by a most favourable omen. During the advance there was an almost continuous rain, a most unusual thing in Upper Burma in the month of November, but an earnest of a fine harvest in the month of February. The Burmese are a very superstitious race, and they will consider this rainfall, which has averted what seemed the certainty of a famine in the country, as a proof that the British arms are supported by the powers of Nature. Such an indication was, however, hardly wanted. We may be sure that they will accept our rule willingly, and that under its influence they will grow prosperous and forget the pride they enjoyed in having a ruler of their own race, however bad he might be.

THEIR FAULTS.

At any rate the Upper Burmans will soon acquire the geniality which is a type of the race, and makes our older British Burmans so popular. They are favourites equally with the freshest griffin ten days landed and with the oldest resident, whose liver has made him testy for many a year. Their very faults lean to virtue's side. They are most marvellously and inconceivably lazy. Energetic people declare that a Burman is good at nothing but steering a boat or driving a bullock cart. But too great laziness is certainly no more objectionable than too systematic plodding. The Chinaman, who grubs money night and day, is not a charming spectacle. In Burma no one can starve, and there is not a beggar to be seen except the poor lepers on the pagoda steps, and the special class who are bound to beggary by birth and religion, and who are often extremely wealthy. The ordinary Burman takes a job at carpentry work, or in the harvest field, to get a little money, and then he does nothing till he has got rid of it all. When he does make a large sum of money, he spends by far the greater part of it on some pious work, and rejoices in the thought that this will meet with its reward in his next existence. If he never gathers together enough to build any great public work, at any rate he subscribes what he can, and is generous in almsgiving to the monks. So he jogs on through a calm and contented existence, the most cheerful of mortals, troubled by no cares, and free from all the temptations of ambition. The other most obvious fault the Burman has is, as we have said, that he is very conceited. His religion and his physical strength and the national literature all tend towards bumptiousness, and whenever a Burman can assert himself he does. He has the most profound contempt for the natives of India, and will not endure being treated otherwise than as an equal, or at any rate a non-dependent, by Europeans. If you hit him, he will hit you back again. If you abuse him, he will justify himself, and retaliate. This is all very well when it does not go too far, but they are frequently absurdly over-touchy, and resent altogether imaginary slights. This, coupled with their extremely unbusiness-like ways, makes them

I

of very little use in offices or houses of business, and they have, therefore, very little to do in the Government departments or in mercantile houses, where the methodical Chinaman or the fawning native of India is a hundred times more useful, if in other respects not so agreeable, to his chiefs. Still, the Burman's sturdy independence is a great attraction in the East, where it is, in other races with whom we have come in contact, so markedly absent.

THEIR VIRTUES.

Some one with a taste for comparisons has called the Burmese "the Irish of the East." In their love of fun and rollicking they certainly resemble "the finest peasantry in the world," and they are quite as ready to break one another's heads for the mere joke of the thing, but they are much too easy-going to bother themselves with demands for Home Rule, or the organization of land or any other leagues. A Burman is always ready to welcome a joke, and not unseldom is able to cap it, while nothing is so remarkable about the natives of India as their utter incapacity to recognize wit, or to appreciate humour that is not of the broadest. The great similarities of sound in a tonic language like the Burmese give abundant opportunity for play on words, and they are therefore very free in the use of the "basis of all wit," and every dramatic piece abounds in puns and plays on words.

One of the most remarkable traits of the people is the complete equality of all classes. They are perfectly republican in the freedom with which all ranks mingle together and talk with one another, without any marked distinction in regard to difference of rank or wealth. One cause of this, no doubt, is that there are no regular working-men ; another, and this is the chief one, is the character of the religion. Buddhism brings all men—all Buddhists, at any rate—down to the same level. The poor man may be a king of spirits in the next life ; the high-placed sinner may frizzle in the awful pains of hell. There is no difference between man and man but that which is established by superiority in virtue. In this they remain true to the most startling teaching of the Great Master, as it is told in " The Light of Asia." The Master had asked for milk from the shepherd's lota :—

"'Ah, my Lord,
I cannot give thee,' quoth the lad, 'thou seest
I am a Sudra and my touch defiles!'
Then the World-honoured spake: 'Pity and need
Make all flesh kin.   There is no caste in blood,
Which runneth of one hue, nor caste in tears,
Which trickle salt with all; neither comes man
To birth with tilka-mark stamped on the brow,
Nor sacred thread on neck.   Who doth right deeds
Is twice-born, and who doeth ill deeds vile.
Give me to drink, my brother; when I come
Unto my quest it shall be good for thee.'"

EXCELLENCE AS BUDDHISTS.

Burmese Buddhism is probably the purest form of that faith existing—the nearest to the teachings of Prince Siddartha, the Buddha Shin Gautama, as he is called in Burma. Every man in the country enters the monastery at some period of his life; enters it not merely as a scholar, for the monasteries are the only national schools, but actually as a member of the holy order.   He shaves his head and wears the yellow robe for a longer or shorter time; for a Lent, perhaps—that is, about four months—or perhaps only for a month, or a week, or even only for a day; but he must enter it with all the formalities of renouncing the world, and he must go at least

once round the village, with the begging-bowl
hung round his neck, with the regular
members of the monastery. Without this he
has not received " Buddhist baptism ;" he has
not attained to "humanity," to the full privi-
leges of a man ; he could not count his present
existence as other than an animal's ; all the
evil he did would swell the sum of his
demerits, but not a single good action, no
uttermost act of charity or devotion, would
be recorded to his advantage in his next
transmigration. Man has less innocence
than the animals, and cannot, like them,
progress by merely omitting to sin.

On entering a monastery, the lad—for
almost all become probationers in their teens
—assumes a new name, which, on the
analogy of Christian, may be called his
Buddhist name. This he retains as long
as he remains in the holy building; when
he leaves, he resumes his worldly name.
This entry into monastic life is, therefore,
certainly the most important event in the life
of a Burman, and it influences the life of the
whole people. Except in the big towns in
our provinces, the great mass of the population get their education in the monastic

schools, before and after their induction.
Teaching is all that the brethren of the order
do for the people. They have no spiritual
powers whatever.   They simply become
members of a holy society that they may
observe the precepts of the Master more perfectly, and all they do in return for the alms
lavished on them by the pious laity is [to
instruct the children in reading, writing, and
the rudiments of religion.   But it is precisely
this moderate amount of teaching, revealing,
as it does, all the stern simplicity of the
monastic life, that keeps Buddhism so active
in the country, and resists the efforts of
Christian missionaries in Burma.   The tone
of the monks is undoubtedly good.   Any in-
fractions of the law, which is extraordinarily
complicated, are very severely punished ; and
if a *pohn-gyce* (or "great glory"), as the
monks are termed, were to commit any
flagrant sin, he would forthwith be turned
out of the monastery to the mercy of the
people, which would not be very conspicuously prominent. Beyond their teaching, the monks act simply as models to the
people.   Buddhism is a very pronounced
form of atheism, notwithstanding the simi-

larity of many of its precepts to Christian doctrine. In a religious system which acknowledges no supreme Deity, it is impossible for any one to intercede with a Creator whose existence is denied on behalf of a man who can only attain to a higher state by his own pious life and earnest self-denial. The religious are, therefore, only higher members of a community in which every individual is striving at a greater degree of sanctity. For this reason the doors of the monastery are always open as well to those who wish to enter as to those who wish to leave it. The longest stayer has the greatest honour.

In return for their self-denial the monks are highly honoured by the people. In Upper Burma all bow down when the mendicant passes, and the women kneel on each side of the road. In our lower provinces such outward marks of respect are not usual in the larger towns, but there is no lack of veneration, and all make way for him when he walks abroad. The oldest layman assumes the title of disciple to the last inducted brother, and with clasped hands addresses him as Payah, the highest title the language affords. The monk's commonest actions, walking, eating, sleeping, are referred to in honorific language different from that which would be used of a layman, or even of the king, performing the same thing. Finally, the *pohn-gyee's* person is sacred and inviolable. Nothing he does can subject him to the civil law. He bears the title of Thageewin Prince, as the heir of the scion of Kapilavastu and receiver of his inheritance.

DOCTRINE OF GOOD WORKS.

Religion pervades Burma in a way that is seen in hardly any other country, perhaps because every one has, at some time, been a monk. No Burman will take animal life, even of the most noxious kind. Stories are told of mothers who have allowed snakes or scorpions, that have bitten their children, to escape unharmed. Our man in the moon is, by the Burmese, changed into a rabbit, because Gautama, when he was on earth in the form of that animal, made a peculiar sacrifice to a previous Buddha. All creatures on earth were bringing presents; the lion brought venison, the hawk dainty birds, the bee honey. The rabbit thought : "What can I offer ? Grass is no use, for I cannot bring enough to make a couch. Therefore I will offer my body to be eaten." For this sacrifice, the form of the rabbit was placed in the moon. The tale naturally recalls that in "The Light of Asia," where the Brahmin resigns his life that the tiger and her cubs may not die of famine. The "duty days," as the days for worship are called—the first and eighth of the crescent moon, the full moon, and the eighth of the waning—are kept a great deal better than Sundays in most Christian countries. On special festivals the pagoda platforms are thronged by crowds varying according to the sanctity of the place, and at no time of the day can you visit any pagoda with a repute for sanctity without seeing some devout people reciting the lauds of the Buddha before the shrines. The number of pagodas in the country is altogether extraordinary. There is no village so poor but that it has its neatly kept shrine, with the remains of others mouldering away round about it. No hill is so steep and rocky, or so covered with jungle, as to prevent the glittering gold or snow-white spire rising up to guard the place from ghouls and sprites, and remind the surrounding people of the Saviour Lord, the teacher of Nirvana and the Law. The banks of the Irrawaddy are lined with them from the source to the northern hills.

There is good reason for this multiplication of fanes. No work of merit is so richly paid as the building of a pagoda. The pagoda founder is regarded as a saint on earth, and when he dies he obtains the last release; for him there are no more deaths. The man who sets up a row of water-pots on a dusty road does well; he who raises a sacred post, who builds a rest-house, presents an image or a bell, or founds a monastery, gains much merit and ensures a happy transincorporation when he passes away; but the *Payah-tagah* is finally freed from the Three Calamities, his merits outweigh the demerits, and he attains the holy rest, if not immediately, at any rate much sooner than a less pious individual. It may be remarked that it is of no avail to repair a previous dedication, unless it be one of the great world-shrines at Rangoon, Pegu, Prome, or Mandalay. In the case of ordinary pagodas the merit of the repair goes not to the restorer, but to the founder. Pagodas are built over relics of the Buddha, or models of them, over the sacred eight utensils of a mendicant, or imitations of these, and over copies of the sacred books.

SUPERSTITIONS.

The Burmese religion thus enters into the life of the people in a much more thorough way than is to be seen in the majority of other lands.

Religious buildings are the most conspicuous things in the country, the only conspicuous buildings indeed, for the Burman's house is a very insignificant erection, usually of bamboo and mats, sometimes of timber, but never of anything more substantial. But, notwithstanding their devotion to Buddhism, they have a great many superstitions derived from the Shamanism which was undoubtedly the faith of their forefathers before Buddhaghosha came among them as an apostle. These heresies are also kept alive by their contact with the spirit-worshipping hill-tribes who surround them.

The most singular of these beliefs is that which affects the naming of the Burmans.

The consonants of the language are divided into groups, which are assigned to the days of the week, Sunday having all the vowels to itself. With all respectable families it is an invariable rule that the child's name must begin with one of the letters belonging to the day on which it was born. For example, a child born on Sunday might be called Shway O, Golden Pot. If it were a boy, it would be called Moung Shway O, Mr. Golden Pot, or, in later days, simply Oo O, Old Pot; if a girl, it would be Mah Shway O, Miss (or Mrs.) Golden Pot.

On Monday the letters are *k*, *g*, and *ng*, or these letters aspirated. Examples: Moung Kway Yoh, Mr. Dog's Bone; Mah Kyit Sway, Miss Loved Darling.

Tuesday: Moung Sehn Nee, Mr. Red Diamond; Mah See, Mrs. Oil.

Wednesday: Moung Bah Wah, Mr. Father Fat; Mee Hla, Miss Pretty.

Thursday: Moung Bah Hmoay, Mr. Father Fragrance; Mah Poo, Mrs. Hot.

Friday: Hpo Thin, Grandfather Learned; Mah Han, Mrs. Haughty.

Saturday: Moung Hpo Too, Mr. Like His Grandfather; Mah Noo, Miss Tender.

Also—corresponding to the English rhyme, "Monday's child is fair of face," and so on—they have a notion that according to the day of the week (or rather the constellation representing that day) on which a man was born, so will his character be. Thus a man born on Friday will be talkative; on Saturday, quarrelsome; on Sunday, parsimonious; and so on. Not only has every day its special character and its fixed letters, but there is some particular animal assigned to symbolize it, and red or yellow wax-candles are made in the forms of these animals to be offered at the pagoda by the pious. Each worshipper offers a creature candle representing his birthday, or that of any particular friend or relation whom he wishes well. In this way Friday is represented by a guinea-pig; Saturday by a dragon; Sunday by a *Kalohn*, the fabulous half-beast, half-bird, which guards the terrace of Mount Meru; Monday by a tiger, and so on. This superstitious idea has considerable ramifications; for example, a man or a woman born on a Friday ought not to marry one born on a Monday. One or other, or both of them, would die if they persisted in marrying one another. Similar unhappy conjunctions are the union of couples born on Saturday and Thursday, or Sunday and Wednesday. Burmese young ladies know all these "hostile days," as they are called, well enough; they are set forth in jingling rhymes, and as they know the day a man is born on by his initial letter, they cut short the supplications of a swain who would rush on his own ruin. On the other hand, there is an elaborate figure to show what unions according to birthdays will be lucky. Sunday and Tuesday, Thursday and Friday, and Monday and Friday are some of these benignant combinations. In addition to this, there are some months in which it is exceedingly unwise to get married. Nevertheless, though there is all this trouble in getting a wife, complications undreamed of by our novel-writers, the Burmese manage to get married very early. Some of them also get married very often, but these are only rich people, and in our lower provinces public opinion is against it, though the law is not.

LUCKY AND UNLUCKY DAYS.

Other notions about luck and ill-luck in connection with days of the week are that Tuesday and Saturday are bad days to do anything. If you commence an extensive work on either of these days, you will soon die. But Thursday is a good day; so is Friday, if you are a student; you will become an authority if you commence your reading on that day. On the other hand, the Burmese believe, as our sailors do, that it is a bad day to begin a voyage. Saturday is a bad day for everything, especially for fires. Washing the head is a very serious matter in Burma, where both men and women have very long locks, not uncommonly, in the women, so long as to trail on the ground. It is therefore as well for them to know that it is unlucky to wash the head on Monday, Friday, or Saturday. Beyond this, men born on certain days are exposed to dangers in particular months. Children born on Wednesday or Friday ought to be very careful what they do in the months of May, September, and January. The best thing is for them to do nothing, and in Burma they act on the precept with great zeal. So it is with other days during other months. On the other hand, there are days which are exceedingly lucky in particular months. Thursday and Saturday are the best days in January, and Thursday and Tuesday in February. It must, however, be remembered that these days are only lucky for those who were born on them, and not for everybody.

Naturally, where there are so many snares awaiting the unwary, there are hosts of professional wizards and fortune-tellers to keep people who can afford to pay for it from getting into trouble. They act as doctors as well as wise men, and deal in cabalistic squares and symbols of the most impressive kind. When a love-sick maiden wants a love-philtre to win back a truant swain, she visits the *Hmaw-sayah*, and gets, along with the draught, a long string of mixed sense and nonsense, which she has to repeat before a figure representing the base, deceiving young man. When a man wants to build a house, he consults the doctor, so that he may know what kind of wood to use, what month to begin it in, and on what day in that month, and what the soil should be like. The doctors, when they have to cure sick people, hark back on the birthday again. There are two sects of these men, the druggists and the dietists. The latter especially affect the birthday nostrum. They will not let a man born on a Sunday eat any article of food whose name begins with a vowel; eggs (*Oo*) and cocoanuts (*Ohn-thee*), for example, are strictly forbidden. Similarly, a Monday's child must refrain from seasoning his curry with ginger (*Gyin-sehn*) or garlic (*Kyet-thohn-byoŏ*), and must avoid any edible whose Burmese name begins with a *k*, a *g*, or an *ng*, or any of these letters aspirated. The druggists are no less astonishing in their specifics. One of them exhibited to an astounded English doctor a green powder nostrum, with the information that it contained a hundred and sixty different ingredients, and was infallible in its results. No doubt it was. The man who could not be affected by one of these ingredients could hardly have been worth curing.

THE MOST SOCIABLE OF MEN.

But under such circumstances the Burmese hardly appear to their advantage. It is on

K

one of the great pagoda feast-days that they
are seen at their best.   Then it is difficult to
say which sex is the more brightly dressed ;
the men with their brilliant turbans and
gorgeous costly silk waistcloths, not unlike a
kilt with a long end, either thrown over the
shoulder or tucked in at the waist, or the
women with their gay neckerchiefs, snowy
white jackets and *tamehns,* or skirts, of
endless pattern and striking contrast of
colour, red or white flowers wreathed in
their jet-black hair, and jewellery in extraordinary profusion.   The sight is one which
is not readily forgotten, and is impossible to
describe.   Wind-stirred tulip-beds, or a stir-
about of rainbows, or a blind man's idea of a
chromatrope are the only suggestions which
can be offered.   After devotion at the pagoda,
there is the meeting with friends from remote
parts of the country, the picnicing in the rest-
houses, and the religious and other plays at
night, when the old people gossip and listen
to the moral declarations from the stage,
while the young people do as much flirting
as can be managed under the circumstances.

They are as hospitable as the traditional
Scotchman, and are fond of the company of

Europeans, although they are inclined to pity them because, not being Buddhists, they are as likely as not to become animals, if not something worse, in another existence. If you enter a remote village in the jungle, where perhaps no white man has ever been seen before, you are sure of a pleasant reception. You may be splashed with the mud of the jungle paths, your clothes ragged from the attacks of wait-a-bit thorns, and your general appearance anything but suggestive of respect, say to the inhabitants of an English village. Your coolies with the provisions and baggage may not have arrived, and there is nothing to show that you are not a mere loafer. No matter ; the first householder you see takes note of nothing except that you are tired and thirsty. One man takes your pony, if you have one, and rubs it down and sees that it has something to eat ; another leads you off to his house and produces a chair or a mat for you to sit on while he gets some refreshments, palm-toddy, or a freshly opened cocoanut, or lemonade or beer, if he has it, and anything more solid that he thinks you are likely to care for. Not until you have refreshed yourself does

K 2

he ask where you have come from and what
your business is.   By this time the headman
of the village has heard of your arrival, and
comes along to pay his respects, and suggests
that you should make use of his house, and
in the evening he probably gets the village
performers together for a concert, or a
country dance, or even a regular dramatic
performance, in your honour.   While you eat,
the master of the house himself will stand at
hand to serve and entertain you, and the
other members of the household will go
outside so that you may be entirely at your
ease.   The perfect freedom of the women,
and the unconstrained way in which they
answer your questions and ask others of you,
is particularly pleasant to an Englishman, and
very different from the state of affairs which
you would find in India or in most other
Indo-Chinese countries.

It is unpleasant to say that this open-
heartedness is very often abused.   Deserters
from British regiments, and sailors who have
left their ships, and the miscellaneous class of
loafing blackguards who are a disgrace to the
British name in the East, are never in want
of a meal or a roof over their heads in the

smallest Burmese village, and might stay for
months without being asked to do a hand's
turn for their maintenance, as long as they did
not get drunk and uproarious, which, as a
matter of fact, they always do. This naturally results in their being requested to go
elsewhere. Nevertheless, however badly his
predecessor may have conducted himself, the
loafer meets with unfailing kindness, even
though he asks for money, as some of them,
lost to all sense of decency, are not ashamed to
do. Charity is the most prominent doctrine of
Buddhism, and the Burmese carry it to extraordinary lengths, but money very few Burmans
have. When they do make a lucky haul with
a judicious paddy speculation, or a *coup* in the
timber trade, they forthwith spend all the
money in works of merit, or in hiring a
wandering troupe of actors for the amusement
of the neighbourhood. Then they are penni-
less and happy again. They have entirely
avoided the curse of Adam, and scout the
necessity of earning their bread with the sweat
of their brow.

It is in their sports that the Burmese are
most energetic. Hunting and shooting they
do not care for, because they imply the

taking of life, and are severely punished in a future life. But in all sorts of games they engage with the greatest enthusiasm, and display a vigour which would do credit to the most energetic of nations. It is enough to say that the Burman goes wild with excitement over boat-races and foot-races and pony-races, that he wrestles and boxes with equal vigour, and that he rejoices in the introduction of English football because, as he says, it is "just like fighting." Unfortunately, he gambles almost as freely as the Chinaman on anything on which money can be staked. Nevertheless, he is an extremely good fellow, manly, good-humoured, and kindly, and the mains of cocks and buffalo-fights in which he delights have none of the brutalities about them which characterize these sports in other countries. Above all, he is sober and abstemious in his way of life, except in a few cases where he has been spoilt by Western example in the coast-ports. It is their natural kindness and that first of all qualifications for the title of gentleman, consideration for the feelings of others, which make the Burmese such general favourites with all who come across them.

FREEDOM OF THE WOMEN.

The freedom which the women enjoy in Burma is not to be paralleled anywhere in the East. All the money and possessions which a girl brings with her on marriage are kept carefully separate for the benefit of her children or heirs, and she carries her property off with her if she is divorced, besides anything she may have added to it in the interim by her own trading or by inheritance. Thus a married Burmese woman is much more independent than any European even in the most advanced States. The Burmese maiden disposes of her affections as she pleases, marries the lad she likes best, and separates herself from him afterwards, if he offends her, by the simple process of going before the village elders and stating her case. If the complaint is just, the request is never refused. The women, though they are not nearly so well educated as their brothers, are nevertheless wonderful managers. A farmer's wife will carry out the sale of the whole rice-crop to the agent of an English rice firm, and generally strikes a better bargain than the farmer would himself. If the village constable is away, his wife will get the policemen together, stop a fight, arrest the offenders and send them off to the lock-up all on her own responsibility. The wife sits by, no matter what business is being transacted, and often puts in her opinion quite as a matter of course. In fact, she is virtual master of the house, and henpecked husbands are not by any means uncommon—King Theebaw was a notable instance.

Courting in Burma is carried on under somewhat singular conditions. The lovers never meet alone. Walks in lovers' lanes, and rendezvous *à quatre yeux* would be looked upon as highly improper, no matter at what hour of the day. There is a fixed hour for the occupation—about nine o'clock at night, which is, therefore, commonly referred to in the country as "lads go courting time." Preparation is duly made by the girl. She gets herself up for conquest, and calls in some friends to support her. The lover, also with a friend or two, comes round at the courting hour and makes his presence known by whistling—an accomplishment at which many Burmans are not by any means proficient. To avoid useless labour in blowing out their cheeks in futile attempts to get to the sounding point, some of them prefer to bring one-stringed fiddles with them, and saw backwards and forwards in a somewhat agonizing way. This he has to do till the girl signals that the old people have gone to bed, for the old people are not allowed to be present in the room, though it is said that the mother has always a crack in the wall through which she can survey operations, and see that the *soupirant* is a suitable personage. When the flirt of a handkerchief has announced that the coast is clear, the lover ascends with his supporters, and they sit down in front of the girls and smoke and philander as much as they can under such conditions. Kissing and caressing are not permitted. Such proceedings a Burmese girl would consider highly indecorous, no matter how many people were looking on. If the parents do not object, a very few meetings of this kind are enough, and the pair are married off with the most ardent-lover-like rapidity. The marriage is a mere civil rite, and depends more upon the publicity of the thing than anything else. All the people of the village, or of the neighbourhood, if it is a large town, are invited to

the bride's house.   The men sit together and
chew betel and drink lemonade and other
sweet drinks and talk for an hour or two, and
the women gather in an inner room and
smoke cigars and discuss matters generally.
Formerly the bride and bridegroom used to
eat rice out of the same dish and feed one
another with morsels in turtle-dove fashion ;
but this has been given up of late years, and
there is really no ceremony at all.   One old
tradition which is still kept up seems to be
the most tangible point in the whole formality.
The young men of the district gather together
after dark and fling stones on the roof of the
happy pair.   Some people imagine that this
is a mere sordid attempt to extort money,
but it has a much more creditable and ancient
origin.   When the primæval Brahmas came
down to this earth, there were nine of them.
As they gradually became deteriorated by
eating gross earthly food, four of them
assumed the form of women and five of men.
Eventually they paired off and married, but
there remained one Brahma an enforced
celibate, and to relieve his feelings he
went and threw stones at the houses of the
blissful new-married couples.   In sympathy

with him, the Burmese bachelors show their envy in a similar way.

Separation is just as simple as the union itself. It is not an easy matter to blame the Burmese for this. The system puts a speedy end to unhappy and ill-assorted unions, and, as a matter of fact, divorces are not common, and the parties are always made the butt of the village wits, and not uncommonly marry one another again when they have thought it over.

A NATION OF SMOKERS.

It is commonly asserted that the Burmese all smoke, and that Burmese babies cry for a cigar instead of crying for the moon. This is not so. Burmese children never smoke before they can walk, but as soon as they can do that they start with cigars that might do as walking-sticks for them. It is quite common to see a lot of little boys and girls in the street making mud-pies and puffing clouds with equal enthusiasm. Burmese cigars are very big, nearly an inch in thickness, and they round a young lady's mouth a little too much perhaps. But they smoke them all the same, and the usual present a Burmese belle makes to the favoured swain is a bundle of cigars rolled by her own fair hands.

CONTENTED WITH BRITISH RULE.

There can be no doubt that the people are satisfied with our rule. They grumble at the taxes, of course, but everybody does that everywhere. Nevertheless, it seems undeniable that our system might be considerably improved. In Lower Burma we have based our land revenue and capitation tax on the old national system as we found it laid down in the codes when we annexed the country. But officers trained in India have modified it according to their Indian experiences, and the result is, perhaps, not very happy. Thus our capitation tax is levied at rates which vary in different districts from one to five rupees, but every householder, rich or poor, has to pay the same. Our land revenue is collected on all cultivated lands at rates varying, according to circumstances, from less than a rupee to five rupees an acre. In Upper Burma there has been theoretically no

land-tax at all. The land-tax is, no doubt,
an admirable form of raising revenue, but the
system does not seem to suit the Burmese,
and one result has been a tendency for the
proprietary right in land to pass into the
hands of money-lenders and capitalists, a fact
which must be very adverse to the well-
being and happiness of the people generally.
The holdings are usually very small. Along
the old frontier they averaged only about five
acres ; in the Rangoon district, from sixteen
to twenty acres. Larger tenancies are, however, entirely against the genius of an easy-
going people like the Burmese, and it would
be a misfortune if our system improved away
the humdrum and lazy, but good-natured and
well-affected, old farmer. In favour of the
capitation tax hardly anything is to be said.
The people pay it dutifully enough, but it is
unjust, because it presses equally upon rich
and poor, on the young man just starting in
trade or in a farm and on the wealthy old
trader or money-lender who lives close by.
Money is so easily got that the grievance
does not become serious ; but if it could be
remitted, or converted into some tax on consumption, the boon would be very consider-

able to the poorer classes. Under our present inelastic system, not only is no exemption granted to the very poor on account of their poverty, and no additional demand made on the rich on account of their wealth, but the traders get off without paying their proper share, for they are much more wealthy than the agriculturists, and they pay little but the capitation tax. If an income-tax, the principle of which exists in the national Burmese system, though it never appeared in reality except as oppression, were established, the general result would be much fairer. Particular care will have to be taken in this respect in our new province, for not only are the people there most abjectly poverty-stricken, but they have no notion of what taxes are collected for unless it be for the special benefit of the rulers. The poverty cannot fail to disappear in so fertile a country, but the people will have to be educated into civilized methods of collecting revenue.

ASCENDENCY OF THE CHINAMAN.

In any case it seems almost certain that, in no very long time, Burma, or at any rate the large trading towns of Burma, will be for all practical purposes absorbed by the Chinese traders, just as Singapore and Penang are virtually Chinese towns, quite as much Chinese as Hong-Kong or the English and American concessions in Shanghai. Unless some marvellous upheaval of energy takes place in the Burmese character, the plodding, unwearying Chinaman is almost certainly destined to overrun the country to the exclusion of the native race. The Burmese do a good deal of trading, but it is in a small, huckstering way, and it is usually carried on by the women. Great numbers keep stalls in the market, or in their houses, who do not at all stand in need of the profits to be made in this way. It is a mere shadow of the great instinctive trading energy of the Chinaman. Proof of this, if it were wanted, would be found in the fact that the women keep all the profits to themselves, usually to be expended in alms for the monks or other pious works. Money is not what is sought after, and without a desire for gains trade cannot flourish to any very great extent. The attraction is usually the gossip of the market-p'ace or of the casual purchaser, the new faces to be seen, and, in the case of young ladies, the openings for flirtation which it offers. The sale of a few packets of pickled tea, or of the lime and betel leaves and areca-nuts for chewing, or of the big green cigars, suggests compliments to the gallant purchaser, and, if it does not do that, at any rate it gives opportunities of enlarging the circle of acquaintance. But beyond this there is almost nothing. In Rangoon and Maulmein there are no Burmese shopkeepers selling anything but the produce of the country, and that in the smallest way—vegetables and rice and various utensils for the pagodas, tapestry work, gongs, and dishes for offerings, and such-like matters. All the large shops that compete with the European stores (and with great success, too) are Chinese. So are the more ambitious ventures in the shape of mercantile houses engaged in the rice and timber and piece-goods trades. Even as clerks in Government offices and places of business, the young Burmans are distanced by their Chinese and Indian rivals. Their extreme touchiness and resentment of fancied slights induce them to resign on the faintest provocation, and then

they have to start afresh at the bottom
of the ladder in some other situation. Besides this, it is rare for them to take a
genuine interest in their work, such as the
Chinaman always does with a view to possible future essays on his own account. The
Indian is much too fond of his position to
risk losing it by remonstrance against no
matter what censures may be passed or unexpected tasks suddenly imposed on him.
On the whole, therefore, it would seem
probable that in no very great time the
Burmese will be almost entirely a rural
population, or at the most only hangers-on
about the great towns. They will live peace-
fully and contentedly on their small farms,
or in little townships remote from the bust-
ling, greedy world. There is probably no-
where in the world at the present time
a population which is so generally well off -
as our low-country Burmans. There are no
very rich people among th :m, but on the
other hand, there are none that do not
support themselves in a very considerable
degree of comfort. Burma is a country that
has never known, and can never know,
famine except as a direct result of civil war

L

and misrule.   It is perhaps a pity that the
Burmese have not more vigour about them,
but, on the other hand, it would be a pity if
so simple and contented and genial a people
were to be spoilt by a new and sordid desire
for the acquisition of wealth.

TRADE.

Burma has been visited by traders as far
back as we can find historical writers.
Indeed, there is not wanting the usual
enthusiast who identifies the country with the
Ophir whence Solomon obtained his gold.
However that may be, Arabs and Chinese and
Indians were succeeded by Portuguese and
Persians, and so the trade has gone on till, at
the present day, nearly every commercial flag
in the world may be seen in Rangoon
harbour, and in the streets are to be seen
natives of every country, from Japan to Russia
and from Sweden to the Pacific coast.

No shipping statistics are to be obtained
earlier than the beginning of the present
century. From 1801 to 1811 the average
number of vessels that cleared out was from
eighteen to twenty-five yearly. In 1822 it

was calculated that the utmost amount of
tonnage likely to find employment annually
between Calcutta and Rangoon was 5400 tons.
After the first Burmese War, from 1826 to
1852, the average annual number of arrivals
and departures was only 125, of which no
more than twenty were European vessels, the
rest being from the Madras coast and China,
coasting schooners, and junks and kattoos.
Heavy duties in kind, at the rate of 12 per
cent., and the conduct of the Burmese autho·
rities acted as a great clog to enterprise.
After the annexation of Pegu in 1856, trade
increased rapidly and has gone on doing so
with hardly any perceptible check. Even
after King Theebaw's accession to the throne
there was an increase in the private export
trade from the United Kingdom into Burma,
as will be seen from the following returns:—

		£
Three years before King Theebaw's accession .	1876–77	4,709,404
	1877–78	4,644,116
	1878–79	5,922,123
Year of accession .	1879–80	5,970,002
Four years after King Theebaw's accession .	1880–81	7,040,640
	1881–82	6,384,893
	1882–83	6,789,635
	1883–84	7,313,451

King Theebaw's misrule did not even
materially reduce the yearly trade between

L 2

British Burma and the upper country, though there were occasional periods of panic, which, however, did not ordinarily last long. The comparative figures are as follow :—

FOUR COMPLETE YEARS BEFORE KING THEEBAW'S ACCESSION.

	Exports from British Burma to Mandalay, &c.	Imports into British Burma from Mandalay, &c.	Total Trade between British Burma and Mandalay, &c.
	£	£	£
1874-75	1,470,261	1,457,572	2,927,833
1875-76	1,355,919	1,514,613	2,870,532
1876-77	1,468,554	1,551,850	3,020,404
1877-78	1,761,541	1,664,385	3,425,926
Average of the four years	1,514,069	1,547,105	3,061,174

AFTER KING THEEBAW'S ACCESSION.

1880-81	1,712,302	1,613,972	3,326,274
1881-82	1,485,886	1,303,375	2,789,261
1882-83	1,581,079	1,670,682	3,251,761
1883-84	1,826,114	1,705,848	3,531,962
Average of the four years	1,651,345	1,573,469	3,224,814

Mr. Bernard, the present Chief Commissioner of Lower Burma, and no doubt destined to be first Lieutenant-Governor of United Burma, in commenting on these statistics, writes as follows to the Government of India :—

" It is perhaps worthy of note that the volume of British trade across our frontier with Ava equals 62 per cent. of the total trade across the whole land frontier of India, from Kurrachee to Chittagong. According to Mr. Hamilton's report for 1881–82, the value of the total trade across the land frontier of India with Biluchistan, Afghanistan, Cashmere, Tibet, Nepal, Sikkim, Bhootan, Manipur, and the tribes of the eastern frontier is valued at about £5,145,000. Our trade with Ava, it has been seen, has averaged £3,224,814 a year during the reign of King Theebaw. To the credit of the Ava Government, it may be mentioned that though the treaty allows them to take a 10 per cent. *ad valorem* import duty on British goods, yet hitherto they have levied only a 5 per cent. import duty. Additional exactions and imports of different kinds are doubtless laid on trade in the interior of the country, and traffic along minor routes in Ava is shackled in many ways. But these obstacles to free commerce would be found in a comparatively uncivilized and comparatively misgoverned State under any circumstances. And the difference between the 10 per cent. duty allowed by treaty and the 5 per cent. duty now levied is, *pro tanto*, a distinct gain to our merchants. During the five years that have passed since the withdrawal of the Resident from Mandalay, the traffic of the Irrawaddy Flotilla Company, probably the largest and wealthiest river navigation company in Asia, has grown and flourished. The increase and the permanence of British trade with Ava is largely due to the exertions and good management of this company."

The nature and amount of the trade of Rangoon from and to all parts will be seen by a glance at the appended extracts from the Customs reports. The commerce with Rangoon so completely overshadows that with other Burma ports that it practically represents the mercantile transactions of the country.

IMPORTS.

Articles.	1883.		1884.	
	3rd Quarter.	4th Quarter.	3rd Quarter.	4th Quarter.
	Rs.	Rs.	Rs.	Rs.
Apparel . .	3,38,139	5,02,079	2,66,559	4,47,513
Cotton twist and yarn . . .	9,92,277	13,80,588	13,38,177	10,27,693
Cotton piece-gds. (including hand-kerchiefs) .	25,23,108	29,25,122	15,82,444	21,96,746
Metals . . .	4,88,793	5,14,478	4,47,030	4,97,136
Oils . . .	3,84,426	5,14,049	8,29,650	6,29,732
Provisions . .	8,58,209	7,10,502	8,19,468	8,91,869
Salt . . .	1,46,639	2,88,566	3,26,376	3,49,117
Silk piece-goods .	9,80,017	15,75,321	15,98,149	22,08,247
Tobacco . .	10,33,965	6,40,464	6,99,400	6,37,325
Woollen piece-gds.	4,81,198	9,36,038	2,80,171	5,68,993
Total trade (including other items not given in detail, but excluding treasure)	1,21,20,748	1,57,01,939	1,20,81,185	1,49,81,089

EXPORTS.

Articles.	1883.		1884.	
	3rd Quarter.	4th Quarter.	3rd Quarter.	4th Quarter.
	Rs.	Rs.	Rs.	Rs.
Caoutchouc, raw .	57,577	23,352	9,665	7,790
Cotton, raw .	4,17,467	3,07,849	1,76,285	2,58,883
Paddy . . .	—	750	—	40,639
Rice . . .	45,38,371	31,25,639	33,93,048	28,69,223
Cutch . . .	3,52,969	6,23,191	3,25,415	5,19,102
Hides, raw . .	3,98,264	3,37,643	5,90,944	4,37,052
Horns . .	28,194	34,835	39,475	.48,216
Oils, mineral .	28,871	59,567	89,709	56,445
Stone, jade . .	2,28,860	1,62,000	2,20,500	—
Tobacco . .	16,314	24,003	23,882	15,057
Wood, teak .	17,65,431	19,52,057	13,79,269	10,28,330
Total trade (including other items not given in detail, but excluding treasure)	83,97,980	71,04,837	67,20,704	57,69,363

The following tables similarly exhibit the nature and amount of the Irrawaddy river traffic to and from Upper Burma :—

IMPORTS.

Articles.	1883.		1884.	
	3rd Quarter.	4th Quarter.	3rd Quarter.	4th Quarter.
	Rs.	Rs.	Rs.	Rs.
Caoutchouc . .	46,782	6,700	32,700	1,800
Chinese and Japanese ware . .	38,845	63,617	52,442	83,493
Cotton, raw .	2,38,669	1,96,805	57,891	1,83,873
Cotton piece-goods (Indian) . .	56,216	1,37,424	38,763	1,33,723
Wheat . .	40,338	10,977	55,187	31,361
Gram and pulse .	98,685	39,720	1,33,797	72,804
Cutch . . .	1,53,258	1,99,888	85,896	1,02,335
Hides of cattle .	1,55,898	1,61,388	3,02,503	2,22,933
Oils . . .	2,97,253	4,19,476	3,27,890	4,83,319
Provisions . .	76,346	80,284	1,17,144	34,496
Silk, manufactured	2,37,824	2,12,916	1,67,937	1,90,680
Stone, jade . .	1,03,520	63,520	1,60,400	—
Sugar, unrefined .	3,30,703	2,23,362	3,50,133	3,61,529
Timber . .	7,283	3,01,891	8,782	5,67,217
Total trade (including other items not given in detail, but excluding treasure)	21,12,058	26,11,265	22,28,492	31,46,006

EXPORTS.

Articles.	1883.		1884.	
	3rd Quarter.	4th Quarter.	3rd Quarter.	4th Quarter.
	Rs.	Rs.	Rs.	Rs.
Twist and yarn (European)	5,96,822	2,90,370	4,70,002	2,93,507
Cotton piece-goods (European)	7,29,752	7,30,812	5,50,907	8,06,410
Earthenware and porcelain	81,262	58,505	95,078	57,573
Rice, husked	1,67,215	4,99,024	13,55,123	6,69,171
Rice, unhusked	5,80,160	38,872	10,79,847	63,234
Metals	1,35,343	92,529	1,37,231	64,690
Oils	36,844	59,050	58,110	83,864
Provisions	5,60,938	2,37,244	4,78,847	3,49,199
Salt	46,826	62,898	1,23,332	75,247
Silk, raw	3,99,021	2,94,186	3,34,305	3,88,395
Silk, manufactured	4,09,121	4,49,621	5,30,477	7,17,584
Betel-nuts	1,39,270	84,026	1,12,541	1,53,198
Sugar, refined	6,077	21,102	12,342	12,490
Woollen piece-goods	46,620	3,00,268	61,022	2,02,943
Total trade (including other items not given in detail, but excluding treasure)	43,40,890	35,32,460	58,04,046	41,74,396

The trade reports of these two years cover the period when Rangoon mercantile matters were at their worst. A great many European firms failed, and there was almost a panic.

Property in Rangoon rapidly declined in value, the municipal revenues showed a heavy falling off, and there were excited statements that trade was irredeemably paralyzed, and that nothing but complete ruin stared the mercantile community in the face. Nevertheless, statistical returns showed on the whole scarcely any difference in trade ; what was lost in one item was gained in another. This was certainly poor consolation to bankrupt merchants. The causes were various, and doubtless the anarchy in Upper Burma was at the bottom of them all. Over-competition and reckless speculation brought down many rice firms trading to Europe. Others had to suspend on account of the numerous serious failures that occurred among Chinese and other native firms who dealt in imported goods and sent British goods to Upper Burma. The disturbed and lawless state of affairs under the king prevented them from realizing their dues from the up-country traders, and they themselves were in their turn unable to meet the liabilities they had contracted with English importing firms. At the same time, paradoxically enough, there was an actual increase in the total value of the trade with Upper Burma during this very period. But this was mainly due to the despatch of a large quantity of rice and paddy to fill the deficit caused by the failure of the food crop in King Theebaw's territories in 1883–84, and this did not help the regular trader at all.

Nevertheless, the fact may be useful as a warning. It is too commonly assumed that the annexation of Upper Burma will result in an immediate and widespread increase to our trade; that we shall find hundreds of new customers, not only in the new province, but beyond in China and in the Shan States, and so on. This is delusive, and may produce a revulsion which would be equally lamentable. The frontier dues are no doubt gone, and therefore manufactured goods can be sold cheaper than before, but, nevertheless, the probability is that the trade up the Irrawaddy will not materially increase for some time. The manufactured silks and worsteds and yarns and cutlery, which the Burmese buy freely, have been sent up country, in spite of the friction between ourselves and the Mandalay Government, in almost as large quantities as are required. It would therefore be a calamity if too great enthusiasm were to lead to an over-accumulation of stocks. It must not be forgotten that the people of Upper Burma as well as of the Shan States, although they are freed, are not less poverty-stricken than they were before, and they cannot become purchasers till they have the means to pay. Wealth is certain to come in time, but it cannot come for some years. The persuasion of the Shans and the Kachyens and the Chins and the Paloungs and half a dozen other hill-peoples, that our rule is just and that we will welcome them to the plains, will be the first preparation for making United Burma the paying country which the lower provinces have now been for years. The new province will almost certainly be no little expense for some years, possibly for a good many years, just as the three lower provinces were. There are no roads whatever, and the construction of these will be a considerable drain on the revenues of India for a longer or shorter period. But the money spent in this way will soon be returned in the purchasing power thus created among our new subjects. Pegu, Arakan, and Tenasserim were a great expense to us at first, but they have come to pay a handsome surplus into the Indian treasury, and the same will be true of Upper Burma. The complaints of the native Indian Press about the burden the new annexation is to be to Indian taxpayers are particularly ungracious, when we consider the actual facts. The surplus revenue of India has, of late years, been mainly extracted from Lower Burma. The table on p. 159, the figures of which are taken from the Administration Report published by the Provincial Government, conclusively proves this.

These figures show a sum of close upon six millions sterling absorbed in eight years by India out of a total revenue of seventeen millions. This seems a fairly heavy contribution to the cost of the Central Government, even if we allow that something has to be returned to India for past expenditure. In the same eight years less than two millions were spent on public works, and this seemed so downright a robbery to the Rangoon community that they began to clamour in 1885 for separation from India. There can be no doubt that this would be in the highest degree inadvisable, but at the same

STATEMENT SHOWING THE DISPOSAL OF THE REVENUE OF BRITISH BURMA, FOR EIGHT YEARS.

Years.	Gross Revenue.	Gross Charges in Civil Department.	Surplus in Civil Department.	Net Public Works Expenditure.	Net Surplus for Military Expenditure and Share of the Cost of Central Government.	Military Expenses.	Net Surplus available for Central Government.
	£	£	£	£	£	£	£
1876–1877	1,766,102	704,941	1,061,161	176,013	885,148	283,339	601,809
1877–1878	1,744,539	668,644	1,075,895	110,738	965,157	270,191	694,966
1878–1879	1,909,915	755,218	1,154,697	163,407	991,290	272,341	718,949
1879–1880	2,149,373	836,322	1,313,051	140,043	1,173,008	381,559	791,449
1880–1881	2,186,430	923,404	1,263,026	217,383	1,045,643	361,623	684,020
1881–1882	2,478,516	967,103	1,511,413	353,991	1,157,422	311,577	845,845
1882–1883	2,505,735	1,070,995	1,434,740	401,441	1,033,299	274,656	758,643
1883–1884	2,639,657	1,144,054	1,495,603	332,466	1,163,137	274,474	888,663
	17,380,267	7,070,681	10,309,586	1,895,482	8,414,104	2,429,760	5,984,344

time it is equally undeniable that it is folly not to develop as rapidly as possible a country which, like Burma, teems with natural wealth.

After thirty years of British rule there are scarcely any roads in the country outside of the chief towns. The only railways are the narrow-gauge line to Prome, a hundred and sixty odd miles long, opened in 1877, and another of nearly the same length to Toung-oo, opened eight years later, and therefore not yet a year old. According to the Administration Report on Indian Railways for 1883–84, the line to Prome during the four years ending in 1883 yielded an average profit per annum of 4·63 per cent. on the capital expended, notwithstanding that the line practically follows the course of the Irrawaddy river, and has to compete with the fine and well-served Flotilla Company's steamers. To Toung-oo there is no opposition of this kind. The river journey is a tedious matter of fourteen days, and the road is a mere jungle path. The probabilities are that this line, therefore, will pay even better.

The Burmese of the lower provinces have proved to be purchasers of British manufactures to a very much larger extent per head of the population than the people of India, who have been so very much longer under our rule. In 1884, it is stated in a petition presented by the London Chamber of Commerce, the annual consumption of British produce and manufactures per head in India was ·16 pounds sterling. In Burma, according to the statement of the Rangoon Chamber of Commerce, "the imports from Great Britain for the official year 1883–84 were £2,830,336, exclusive of imports *via* Calcutta. In the Administration Report for that year, the population of British Burma is estimated at 4,334,000 persons, giving a consumption per head of ·65 pounds sterling, or four times that of India. It is true that part of these imports are actually consumed in Upper Burma and the Shan States; but some of the imports to Indian ports also find their way beyond the frontier. The native of India buys little else from the manufacturers of Great Britain than a few yards of cotton cloth. The people of Burma all spend their money freely on imported luxuries."

The potential wealth in Upper Burma,

M

not to speak of Western China, the Shan States, and Karennee, is simply incalculable. We have now the means of opening them up to our trade by railways and roads, and a failure to do so as fast as it can be done would be very short-sighted policy. The money expended on these works would at one and the same time reassure the people, pacify the country, and give the inhabitants the purchasing power they stand in need of.

Upper Burma is, undoubtedly, more fertile and promising than our older provinces. Wheat and other grains and pulse, cutch, gums and resins, lac, petroleum, silk, sugar, tea, tobacco, and timber have long been exported; and with a properly governed country and a contented population, the amount of these must inevitably and enormously increase. The mineral wealth of these regions is probably what will attract speculators most, and a few details concerning this may not be out of place.

Gold is found in small quantities in the Shway-gyeen district of Lower Burma, and on the upper waters of the Irrawaddy and Chin-dwin, as well as of other rivers in the north of Burma. The amount, however, is not great; and most of the gold-leaf so abundantly used on the pagodas and images comes from Yünnan and Ssu-ch'uen. Platinum, called by the Burmese *Shway Pyoo*, "white gold," also appears in the same districts with the exception of Shway-gyeen.

In this latter district also, as well as in various parts of the Shan States, ores of antimony, lead, iron, and copper are found. The Shans are noted blacksmiths, and do a great deal of ironwork, mostly in the form of swords and spear-heads. There are also rude blast-furnaces in the neighbourhood of the iron-mines at the Pohppa mountain, east of Myin-gyan. Much silver is brought down by the Kachyens from their hills to Bhamô and other northern towns. Other regions in the hilly Shan country to the south are also spoken of as being rich in this metal, traces of which are also said to have been seen in the Shway-gyeen district.

Tin is found in the Tenasserim province, and has been worked by an English company at Malawoon. The workings, however, were given up, and are now in the hands of Chinamen, who make a good thing out of them.

M 2

The coal-fields of the Tenasserim province have been reported on at length by Dr. Oldham, Dr. Helfer, and Major-general Tremenheere. The first-named gentleman refers the seams to the Tertiary period of geology, and describes them as "either slaty or conchoidal pitch coal, or English cannel coal, highly bituminous, without any concomitant of iron pyrites." No attempt has, up to now, been made to work the coal in this part of the country. In Upper Burma, however, coal is found on the Irrawaddy itself, and has long been worked by the Burmese. The chief mines are at Thinkadaw on the Irrawaddy, about thirty miles or so above Myin-gyan; also at Shway-goo, old Pagán, and Sheen-pagah, about half-way between Mandalay and Bhamô; and in the Shan hills east of Mandalay. The coal is said to be somewhat light and bituminous, and that in the Shan hills bears a very high character.

Great quantities of amber come from the country north of Bhamô, and this commodity is very abundant and cheap in the Mandalay bazaars. It is largely used for ear-tubes, rosaries, necklaces, and similar ornaments by the Burmese. The principal source of the supply is Payen-toung, a hundred and fifty miles or so north of Bhamô.

No small quantity of jade is also worked at Mhin-khoon on the Moh-goung river, a region known as the Burmese Siberia. Most of it is sent to China, where jade is held in higher estimation than most metals.

The ruby-mines of Burma are especially celebrated. Rubies were the monopoly of the kings of the country, and no Englishmen were ever allowed to go near the mining districts. A French engineer, a Mons. Bonvillain, is reported to have inspected the most wealthy deposits, which are at Kyay-pyin, Kha-thai, and Moh-goht, about seventy miles to the north-west of Mandalay, and to have proposed to lease them for a period of four years, paying thirteen lakhs of rupees for the concession. The precious stones are found in an extensive bed of gravel at no great distance below the surface, and, besides rubies, topazes and emeralds are found in some quantities. There are also less productive mines close to Mandalay in the Sa-gaing hills.

Everything, in fact, conspires to show that

Burma is the most valuable addition to our empire made for many years. The abundance of rich land, the facility with which rights over it can be acquired, the great demand for rice and the ever-increasing counter-demand for European manufactured goods, the cessation of all irregular and unexpected collections, the absolute security enjoyed by all under the British Administration—all these benefits · have resulted in trebling the population of the lower provinces since we took charge of them ; in the more than trebling of the trade, the value of the sea-borne merchandise alone having doubled and reached thirteen millions sterling during the last ten years; and in the wonderful increase of revenue, which has made Burma hitherto the most valuable of all the provinces — under the Indian Government, a position which it cannot fail to maintain now that its troublesome neighbours have been turned into contented subjects.

HILL-TRIBES.

Allusion has been made in the earlier pages of this book to the great numbers of wild tribes to be found scattered throughout the hills of Burma. At the first blush, if one were to believe the report of the peoples themselves, and more particularly the names they give themselves, it might appear that the country was a veritable hotch-potch of nationalities. But a closer examination of dialects, and especially of traditions and customs, proves that, as a matter of fact, they are merely waifs and strays from the four main stocks already noticed. They may call themselves Chyens, Kyaws, Kyoungthahs, Paloungs, Toungthahs, Khamis, Mros, Shandoos, Yabehns, Pwos, Shyoos, and a score of other names, but they do not represent the absolute chaos the list of their appellations hints at. It is true that the Salones of the Mergui Archipelago, some of the Arakan — hill-tribes, and the Kachyens of the north are entirely different in race from the Burmese, Peguan, Karenn, or Shan stocks, but the others are not by any means so isolated as they would make themselves out to be.

It is only the laborious condition of their lives and the bullying to which they have been subjected by Burmese officials that have reduced them to their present wretched state.

To support themselves they have to shift their settlements every few years. Rice can be grown on the flat plain-lands year after year with never diminished return, and no greater labour than is implied in the turning loose of a number of buffaloes or oxen to poach up the saturated grounds with their hoofs—an easy substitute for ploughing, which exactly suits the Burman's lazy temperament. But on the steep hill-slopes it is a very different matter. There the shrub-growth and the trees grow fast and dense, and the rains of the monsoon wash away all the mould that is not held together by vegetable growth of some kind; and, further than this, the soil is so exhausted by a single crop that it must lie fallow for years—from four to seven—before it can raise another harvest. Therefore, when the cold winter months are drawing to a close, each villager selects the strip of ground which he proposes to cultivate, and sets about cutting down the jungle on it. It is toilsome work in any case, but perhaps least so when the trees are of a fair growth. This would seem rather paradoxical to a German forester, but the ingenuity of the highlanders has been developed by the painful experience of generations. They cut a slight notch on the under side of the bottom row of trees, and proceed upwards, for the clearing is always on an incline, cutting gradually deeper and deeper into the trunks, and leaving, as a rule, the smaller trees untouched, until they come to the top of their allotment. There the tree-stems are completely cut through and fall on those below, snap them over, and so the process goes on until the whole acre or so of forest-growth goes down in one huge swaith. Even with this lightening of the toil it takes many days; but by the end of April the jungle has been cut long enough to be dry and ready for burning. Then the heap is kindled, and the hills far and near are lit up with the gleam of the great bonfires. The ashes fertilize the ground, but sometimes the rains come too soon, and wash away half of the pitiful manure and leave large half-burnt logs cumbering the ground, which have to be painfully dragged away by the cultivator and his family. Therefore, he has to be a meteorologist as well as a woodman that he may be able to judge the best time to set fire to his pile of wood.

However, when the timber is burnt and the rains have come, the whole field has to be laboriously hoed up so as to mix in the ash-manure, and then comes the sowing. In some fortunate districts this can be done broadcast; but far more frequently a separate hole into which a rice-grain may be dropped has to be carefully dibbled. After a short time, when the young plants have sprung up a little above the surface, Indian corn, cotton, and capsicums are planted between the ridges, to serve as a last resource in case the cotton-crop should fail; and near the wooden hut, with its low-thatched eaves, crouching under the lee of a protecting rock, there are yams, their tendrils creeping over some blocks of wood placed there for the purpose; a row or two of sugar-canes, somewhat stringy and sapless in such uncongenial ground; some taro, perhaps, if there is a mountain brook near; a few poppies to supply opium; and a line of betel-vines to supply the leaf wherein to wrap the areca-nut, the fragment of tobacco and cutch, and the smear of lime which will, when chewed, furnish comfort and consolation to the farmer if all does not go well.

Even with the sowing, the husbandman's labours are not always over. Sometimes the rains are only partial or intermittent, and the parched soil refuses to produce even one year's crop without irrigation. Then artificial channels have to be dug and conducted through the clearing, and infinite care is necessary to prevent the water carrying off earth, crop, and everything down the steep incline. When the grains begin to swell in the ear, the farmer has to watch day and night against feathered and footed marauders. By day, flocks of screeching green parrots and voracious buntings hover about the little field, and by night herds of wild hogs and deer would soon root up or devour the provision for the year. Then at last, in September or October, the harvest is reaped, the sickle used being as often as not the *dah*, the square-tipped, heavy-bladed sword with which the trees were cut down in the early part of the year. The grain is thrashed out by the laborious process of beating the ears against a log of wood laid on a bamboo-mat, or by the even more irksome method of trituration with the naked feet. Then, at the end of the year, the highlanders pay visits to the low country, carrying down fowls and pigs (in baskets on their backs), wild honey and bees'-wax, wild cardamoms, betel-nuts, and whatever else their hill-tops supply. With the proceeds of their sale they make what small purchases they can—a little more rice perhaps, some cheap finery for their women-folk, and a few spare clothes against the cold winter nights. The winter is, however, their pleasantest time, for then they can idle for a bit and, if they have had a successful season, occasionally indulge in carousals with *khoung* or *sheroo*—heady liquors brewed from fermented rice, and occupying a kind of debateable ground between beer and spirits.

But when the winter is gone, the whole labour begins over again, and, after a year or two, the whole community has to migrate to a new locality. It is this continual moving about, and the necessary isolation in which each settlement dwells, that have produced the dialectic differences which make inter-course with the hill-nomads so difficult a matter. The new site is determined in various superstitious ways. Each head of a household goes away separately, and brings back with him a clod of earth from what he thinks a favourable spot. When all have returned, the explorers place the clod under their pillow at night, and await auspicious dreams. These are communicated to the village synod, and are solemnly considered according to the canons laid down by ancient tradition, and the most promising dream settles the direction of the migration. Occasionally the dreams are not satisfactory, or it is difficult to decide between two or three equally tempting claims. Then a fowl is cooked, and eaten with great formality by the pioneers. The bones are picked clean—the mountain air induces healthy appetites—and then they are broken and thrown into an earthenware jar. This is covered with a cloth, and each house-father picks out a fragment. The one who draws out the biggest has the honour of leading the community to its next dwelling-place. This is seldom very far from the old habitation. One range of hills ordinarily serves as the locality for each particular sept during many generations.

Their Religion.

In their beliefs these nomads are Nature-worshippers of a somewhat random and equivocal kind.　When they are prosperous, they practically worship nothing at all.　Sometimes when they are wandering through the jungle on a hunting or trapping excursion, or in quest of the roots and leaves with which they make messes to eke out the rice-supply, they may here and there tie down the top of a bamboo shoot and deposit a few humble offerings of flowers and fruit to the spirit guardian of the woods; or they may fix upon a particular tree, some great forest-giant, or some rare species, as the abode of a *Nat*, and make propitiatory signs, or mutter a few prayers; but they have no regular religious services, though they are in constant fear of the ghostly inhabitants of the cliffs and trees and streams.　It is only when they fall upon bad times that they indulge in any organized system of devotion.　They ascribe their misfortunes to the anger of the demons, either on account of neglect, or of some particular offence against their dignity.　The two spirits most generally recognized and appealed to on these occasions are the *Nat* of the forest and the hills and the *Nat* of the village. To these, pigs and fowls are sacrificed, libations of rice-beer are poured out, flowers and fruit and cooked rice are offered, a tiny hut or two is built for them in the branches of a tree, and there are many prostrations and noisy incantations. Nevertheless, in spite of the intermittent character of their adorations, they are careful never to run the risk of offending any satyr or dryad. When they make a clearing, they always leave a tree or two standing so that there may be a dwelling-place for the local *Nat*, who, if he were evicted, would inevitably revenge himself, not only on the reckless cultivator, but on the entire community. Not unseldom, prayers and incantations are scratched on the tree-trunks to soothe the disturbed demon, and lull him into acquiescence in the new conditions of his haunts. But the spirits are not held in anything like real reverence. They are all considered to be evil-minded and malicious. The worship, what there is of it, is entirely deprecatory. No one wants the *Nats*, however easy-going they might be. If there were any method of getting rid of them it would forthwith be adopted, for the spirits never do any good except in the negative kind of way of preventing others of their kind, or strangers of earthly birth, from encroaching on their domains and possibly doing mischief. Consequently, hill religious principles are not by any means strongly developed.

Hope for the Nomads.

Ordinarily, these highlanders are meek, harmless, broken-spirited people, who are too hard-worked to have any time for interfering with their neighbours, and have no more hearty wish than to be let alone. Under Burmese rule, they were often seized and sold into slavery, and many villages died of famine or pestilence rather than face the greater danger of falling into the hands of one of King Theebaw's officials. Nowadays, with a just and settled rule, they may be tempted to come down from their eyries and settle in the plains, where they will be relieved from the hardships of long years, and we shall gain industrious and peaceable citizens. Nevertheless, in spite of their weakness whether for offence or defence, the hill-tribes are proud of their traditions. They look upon the inhabitants of the low-lands as inferior people, "lower-born" in the physical sense of the word, descendants of the hillmen, and with no claim to their antiquity, or to their nearness to the heavens, whence came the fallen spirits from whom they believe all mankind to be descended. Still, when it comes to a decision between race-pride and a comfortable life in the level country under English rule, ancestral dignity will probably give way.

The Kachyens.

The Kachyens are a very different set of people. They are hillmen too, but they do not care for hard work. They find it infi-nitely easier and more pleasant to plunder their neighbours. Long ago they are repre-sented as having been a simple people, hospitable to strangers, and inclined to be peaceable with all men. But constant extor-tion and brutal treatment on the part of local governors have turned them into reiving caterans. They were supposed to be tribu-

N

tary to the Burmese king on the one hand
and the Chinese on the other; but it is
long since either have got tribute-money
or homage out of them. They were much
more apt to "lift" cattle and loot caravans,
to drive off fat beeves and steal everything
that was not too hot nor too heavy from low-
land villages. The Chinese walled towns
and train-bands were able to hold their own,
but it is many years since there has been any
neighbourliness between the mountain reivers
and the Burman villagers. Intercourse has
been confined to perpetual warfare, chequered
by crucifixions. Nevertheless, the Kachyens
form an admirable neutral State—if they
can be called a State—between China and
Burma.

The very name Kachyen, given to them
by the Burmese and adopted by all the
surrounding nations, is an outrage on their
feelings. They call themselves Singhpo
or Singpaw, which means "men." They
are the true men; the lowlanders are the
mere bye-blows of degenerate highlanders.
Ethnologically, they are simply a branch of
the vast horde of "Singhpos" proper, who
inhabit the northern Assam hills, and are

better known to us by their local names of
Gáros and Nagas. These truculent tribesmen have, after better acquaintance with us,
settled down into peaceable neighbours, and
it may be hoped that the Kachyens will do
the same. This southern branch of the race
is mixed up with Kakoos and Shans and
other tribes, and trends down into Upper
Burma as far as the hills permit of it. The
farthest south of the Kachyen clans is about
in the latitude of Tagoung, one of the most
ancient Burmese capitals, about half-way
between Mandalay and Bhamô. Those of
the race who have settled in Hookong and
Assam attach great importance to the
name of Singhpo, and call their eastern
and southern brethren " Kachyens " and
" Kakoos " as a term of reproach. The
tribesmen in the neighbourhood of Bhamô
have therefore no very friendly neighbours,
and of late years they have scorned all
attempts at conciliation, and have degene-
rated more and more into dangerous savages.
It is pointed out with considerable show of
reason that the Kachyens are probably the
" Gold-teeth " of whom Ser Marco Polo
writes ; if so, they have long since lost the

wealth and civilization—if it can be called such—which led them to adopt the singular custom of casing their incisors.

A Kachyen village is always as nearly as possible on the top of a mountain peak, either in a sheltered glen near a spring, or straggling loosely up a gentle incline on what the Scotch would call the "lown" side of the summit. There is only one path up to the village, winding up the boulder- and jungle-covered hill-sides, and it is not every village that will admit a stranger. The few Europeans that have visited them have, however, always been well received. · For years no Burman has ventured so much as to set his foot on a Kachyen hill. A peculiarity of the Kachyen village is the formal avenue which always leads into it. This is lined with bamboo posts at short distances, with taller poles at intervals, joined together with rattan cords suspending bamboo stars and circles and other emblems over the roadway. The avenue is usually about a couple of hundred yards long, and at the end nearest the village there are wooden knives and axes and spears and swords fastened to the tree-trunks. All these symbols and models

are for the benefit of the woodland and other
spirits, of whom the Kachyens stand in great
awe. Like the Chinese, they do not give
these demons credit for great wisdom or
acuteness. For one thing, they believe that
they can only move in a straight line. Therefore, the *Nats* avoid going about in the
depths of the jungle, and keep to the open
paths. A few judicious turns are made in
the avenue so as to throw the prowling devil
off if possible, but, if he should happen to be
cannoned off the tree-stems in the right
direction, there are the emblems to show
him where the things he is in search of may
be found. If he is hungry, there is the
bullock's skull nailed to a tree to indicate
where food may be found; if he is thirsty,
a joint of bamboo points out where a libation
of rice-spirit has been made; if he is more
dainty, a conventional sign leads him to
flowers and fruit; if he has a grudge against
a fellow-devil, the spears and swords and
knives are there ready for him. The
Kachyens cordially object to the spirits, and
devote all their ingenuity to keeping them
out of the way. There is a *Nat* in each
house, and for him a special door is re-

served, used only by him and by the household. A stranger entering by this door would be as likely as not be made the immediate propitiatory sacrifice to the offended domestic devil. For the house spirits, though perhaps a shade more enlightened than the jungle ghosts, are still very dense, and might very well wreak their vengeance on one of the household instead of on the offending visitor.

The houses are long low barrack- or shed-like constructions, with thatched roofs coming down all round close to the ground to prevent the hill-storms from dismantling the place. They stand on low piles. A ladder leads to the one long room which constitutes the habitation. A few partitions, cutting off sections not unlike cattle-stalls, form the sleeping apartments, and there are no doors to these. The fireplace stands on the other side. It is simply a range of bricks laid on the bamboo floor, and there is no semblance of a chimney or of windows, so that the wood-smoke causes a good deal of ophthalmia. The cattle and pigs and dogs and fowls live amicably below the house, and do not at all interfere with the comfort of the inmates over their heads.

Each village or township has its own chief, or *Pawmaing*, and there are thus hundreds of independent princelings scattered along the hill-range. When the community becomes too large, the eldest son of the chieftain selects a number of followers and goes off to form a village on a hill of his own. Such settlements are naturally on terms of friendship with the parent village. Otherwise, the hillmen fight among one another like wild cats. They carry guns of their own manufacture—curious things without stocks and fired from the cheek. These, however, are used more for the intimidating noise they make than with any notion that they are valuable for killing people or game. The Kachyen's true weapon is his *dah*, a formidable sword worn in a half-sheath, suspended by a rattan sash over the shoulder. That weapon flashes out on the slighest provocation, and is used with unfailing skill for all purposes—from paring the finger-nails to cutting off a fellow-creature's head. A Kachyen will allow no stranger, even in a village, to pass him on the left or sword side. A brandished *dah* or a savage slash will soon remind the careless man of the impropriety of his conduct.

Notwithstanding their present lawlessness, there is no doubt the Kachyens can soon be reclaimed by kind treatment. Even of recent years they have always carried on a certain amount of trade with the Burmese towns, using as intermediaries the inhabitants of the Shan or Burmese-Shan villages at the foot of the hills. To these, immunity from attack was accorded in consideration of their services as go-betweens. Pigs, sulphur, iron, and silver were the usual commodities sent down by the hillmen; and, in addition to edible luxuries, the chief purchases they made were Birmingham knives and looking-glasses, beads for their women, and woven stuffs for themselves. They have strong commercial instincts, and there is very little doubt but that we shall find them not such bad neighbours after all. They are particularly useful as forming a neutral band between us and China, and it is not at all impossible that in time we may form them into as good military policemen, or soldiers even, as the Goorkhas of Nepaul.

PRINTED BY BALLANTYNE, HANSON AND CO.
LONDON AND EDINBURGH

𝔄 Selection

FROM

𝔐r. 𝔯edway's 𝔓ublications.

GEORGE REDWAY,

15, YORK STREET, COVENT GARDEN, LONDON,

1886.

15, York Street, Covent Garden,

London, *January*, 1886.

Nearly ready.

Sultan Stork,

And other Stories, Sketches and Ballads.

BY

WILLIAM MAKEPEACE THACKERAY.

Now First Collected.

———

None of these pieces are included in the two recently published volumes issued by Messrs. Smith, Elder, and Co.

———

With an Appendix containing the Bibliography of Thackeray (first published in 1880), in a revised and enlarged form.

———

CONTENTS.

———

GEORGE REDWAY, YORK STREET, COVENT GARDEN.

In crown 8vo., in French grey wrapper.   Price 6s.

A few copies on Large Paper.   Price 10s. 6d.

The Bibliography of Swinburne;

A BIBLIOGRAPHICAL LIST, ARRANGED IN CHRONOLOGICAL ORDER, OF THE PUBLISHED WRITINGS IN VERSE AND PROSE

OF

ALGERNON CHARLES SWINBURNE,

(1857-1884).

This Bibliography commences with the brief-lived *College Magazine*, to which Mr. SWINBURNE was one of the chief contributors when an undergraduate at Oxford in 1857-8. Besides a careful enumeration and description of the first editions of all his separately published volumes and pamphlets in verse and prose, the original appearance is duly noted of every poem, prose article, or letter, contributed to any journal or magazine (*e.g., Once a Week*, *The Spectator*, *The Cornhill Magazine*, *The Morning Star*, *The Fortnightly Review*, *The Examiner*, *The Dark Blue*, *The Academy*, *The Athenæum*, *The Tatler*, *Belgravia*, *The Gentleman's Magazine*, *La République des Lettres*, *Le Rappel*, *The Glasgow University Magazine*, *The Daily Telegraph*, etc., etc.), whether collected or uncollected. Among other entries will be found a remarkable novel, published in instalments, and never issued in a separate form, and several productions in verse not generally known to be from Mr. SWINBURNE's pen. The whole forms a copious and it is believed approximately complete record of a remarkable and brilliant literary career, extending already over a quarter of a century.

** ONLY 250 COPIES PRINTED.

GEORGE REDWAY, YORK STREET, COVENT GARDEN.

HINTS TO COLLECTORS

OF ORIGINAL EDITIONS OF

THE WORKS OF

William Makepeace Thackeray.

BY

CHARLES PLUMPTRE JOHNSON.

Printed on hand-made paper and bound in vellum. Crown 8vo., 6s.

*The Edition is limited to five hundred and fifty copies,
twenty-five of which are on large paper.*

———

" . . . . A guide to those who are great admirers of Thackeray, and are collecting first editions of his works.   The dainty little volume, bound in parchment and printed on hand-made paper, is very concise and convenient in form; on each page is an exact copy of the title-page of the work mentioned thereon, a collation of pages and illustrations, useful hints on the differences in editions, with other matters indispensable to collectors. . . . . Altogether it represents a large amount of labour and experience."—*The Spectator.*

"Those who remember with pain having seen the original yellow backs o Thackeray's works knocked to pieces and neglected years ago, may be recommended to read Mr. C. P. Johnson's 'Hints to Collectors.'"—*The Saturday Review.*

" . . . . Mr. Johnson has evidently done his work with so much loving care that we feel entire confidence in his statements. The prices that he has affixed in every case form a valuable feature of the volume, which has been produced in a manner worthy of its subject-matter."—*The Academy.*

"The list of works which Mr. Johnson supplies is likely to be of high interest to Thackeray collectors. His preliminary remarks go beyond this not very narrow circle, and have a value for all collectors of modern works."—*Notes and Queries.*

" . . . . It is choicely printed at the Chiswick Press; and the author, Mr. Charles Plumptre Johnson, treats the subject with evident knowledge and enthusiasm. . . . It is not a Thackeray Bibliography, but a careful and minute description of the first issues, with full collations and statement of the probable cost. . . . Mr. Johnson addresses collectors, but is in addition a sincere admirer of the greatest satirist of the century."—*Book-Lore.*

" . . . . This genuine contribution to the Bibliography of Thackeray will be invaluable to all collectors of the great novelist's works, and to all who treasure an 'editio princeps' the account here given of the titles and characteristics of the first issues will form a trustworthy guide. . . . The special features which will enable the purchaser at once to settle any question of authenticity in copies offered for sale are carefully collated."—*The Publisher's Circular.*

———

GEORGE REDWAY, YORK STREET, COVENT GARDEN.

HINTS TO COLLECTORS

OF ORIGINAL EDITIONS OF

THE WORKS OF

Charles Dickens.

BY

CHARLES PLUMPTRE JOHNSON.

Printed on hand-made paper, and bound in vellum.

Crown 8vo., 6s.

The Edition is limited to five hundred and fifty copies, fifty of which are on large paper.

" Enthusiastic admirers of Dickens are greatly beholden to Mr. C. P. John-son for his useful and interesting 'Hints to Collectors of Original Editions of the Works of Charles Dickens' (Redway). The book is a companion to the similar guide to collectors of Thackeray's first editions, is compiled with the like care, and produced with the like finish and taste."—*The Saturday Review.*

"This is a sister volume to the ' Hints to Collectors of First Editions of Thackeray,' which we noticed a month or two ago. The works of Dickens, with a few notable 'Dickensiana,' make up fifty-eight numbers . . . . and Mr. Johnson has further augmented the present volume with a list of thirty-six plays founded on Dickens's works, and another list of twenty-three published portraits of Dickens. As we are unable to detect any slips in his work, we must content ourselves with thanking him for the correctness of his annotations. It is unnecessary to repeat our praise of the elegant *format* of these books. . . . ."—*The Academy.*

" These two elegantly produced little books, printed on hand-made paper and bound in vellum, should be welcomed by the intending collector of the works of the two authors under treatment, and the more experienced biblio-grapher will find the verbatim reproductions of the original title-pages not without use. . . . . For the purpose of checking the correct numbers of these illustrations, verifying the collations, and detecting possible frauds . . . Mr. Johnson's books are unique. The 'Hints,' moreover, incorporated in his prefaces. . . . and the ' Notes' appended to each entry are serviceable, and often shrewd ; indeed, the whole labour, evidently one of love, bestowed upon the books is exceptionally accurate and commendable, and we hope to welcome Mr. Johnson at no distant date as a bibliographer of a more preten-tious subject."—*Time.*

GEORGE REDWAY, YORK STREET, COVENT GARDEN.

In crown 8vo., 2 vols., cloth.   Price 6s.

The Valley of Sorek.

BY

GERTRUDE M. GEORGE.

With a Critical Introduction by RICHARD HERNE SHEPHERD.

"There is in the book a high and pure moral and a distinct conception of character. . . . The *dramatis personæ* . . . . are in reality strongly individual, and surprise one with their inconsistencies just as real human beings do. . . . There is something powerful in the way in which the reader is made to feel both the reality and the untrustworthiness of his (the hero's) religious fervour, and the character of the atheist, Graham, is not less strongly and definitely conceived. . . . It is a work that shows imagination and moral insight, and we shall look with much anticipation for another from the same hand."—*Contemporary Review.*

"The characters are clearly defined, the situations are strong, and the interest evoked by them is considerable.   The women in particular are admirably drawn."—*Athenæum.*

"Henry Westgate, the hero, is a study of no slight psychological interest. . . . It is the development of this character for good and for evil, through the diverse influence of friends and circumstances . . . . that Miss George has portrayed with singular vigour and skilful analysis. . . . It is impossible to read this story without wonderment at the maturity and self-restraint of its style, and at the rare beauty and pathos, mingled with strength, which mark every page."—*Literary World.*

GEORGE REDWAY, YORK STREET, COVENT GARDEN.

In demy 8vo., with Illustrative Plates.   Price 1s.

Chirognomancy;

Or, Indications of Temperament and Aptitudes Manifested by the Form and Texture of the Thumb and Fingers.

BY

ROSA BAUGHAN.

"Miss Baughan has already established her fame as a writer upon occult subjects, and what she has to say is so very clear and so easily verified that it comes with the weight of authority."—*Lady's Pictorial.*

GEORGE REDWAY, YORK STREET, COVENT GARDEN.

An édition de luxe, in demy 18mo.   Price 1s.

Confessions of an English Hachish Eater.

"There is a sort of bizarre attraction in this fantastic little book, with its weird, unhealthy imaginations."—*Whitehall Review.*

"Imagination or some other faculty plays marvellous freaks in this little book."—*Lloyd's Weekly.*

"A charmingly written and not less charmingly printed little volume. The anonymous author describes his experiences in language which for picturesqueness is worthy to rank with De Quincey's celebrated sketch of the English Opium Eater."—*Lincolnshire Chronicle.*

"A weird little book. . . . The author seems to have been delighted with his dreams, and . . . . carefully explains how hachish may be made from the resin of the common hemp plant."—*Daily Chronicle.*

"To be added to the literature of what is, after all, a very undesirable subject. Weak minds may generate a morbid curiosity if stimulated in this direction."—*Bradford Observer.*

"The stories told by our author have a decidedly Oriental flavour, and we would not be surprised if some foolish individuals did endeavour to procure some of the drug, with a view to experience the sensation described by the writer of this clever brochure."—*Edinburgh Courant.*

GEORGE REDWAY, YORK STREET, COVENT GARDEN.

Monthly, One Shilling.

Walford's Antiquarian :

A Magazine and Bibliographical Review.

EDITED BY

EDWARD WALFORD, M.A.

** *Volumes I. to VII., Now Ready, price 8s. 6d.*

GEORGE REDWAY, YORK STREET, COVENT GARDEN.

THE ONLY PUBLISHED BIOGRAPHY OF JOHN LEECH.

An édition de luxe in demy 18mo.   Price 1s.

John Leech,

ARTIST AND HUMOURIST.

A Biographical Sketch.

BY

FRED. G. KITTON.

New Edition, revised.

"In the absence of a fuller biography we cordially welcome Mr. Kitton's interesting little sketch."—*Notes and Queries.*

"The multitudinous admirers of the famous artist will find this touching monograph well worth careful reading and preservation."—*Daily Chronicle.*

"The very model of what such a memoir should be."—*Graphic.*

GEORGE REDWAY, YORK STREET, COVENT GARDEN.

Third Edition, newly revised, in demy 8vo., with Illustrative Plates. Price 1s.

The Handbook of Palmistry,

Including an Account of the Doctrines of the Kabbala.

BY

R. BAUGHAN,

AUTHOR OF "INDICATIONS OF CHARACTER IN HANDWRITING."

"It possesses a certain literary interest, for Miss Baughan shows the connection between palmistry and the doctrines of the Kabbala."—*Graphic.*

"Miss Rosa Baughan, for many years known as one of the most expert proficients in this branch of science, has as much claim to consideration as any writer on the subject."—*Sussex Daily News.*

"People who wish to believe in palmistry, or the science of reading character from the marks of the hand," says the *Daily News,* in an article devoted to the discussion of this topic, "will be interested in a handbook of the subject by Miss Baughan, published by Mr. Redway."

GEORGE REDWAY, YORK STREET, COVENT GARDEN.

EBENEZER JONES'S POEMS.

In post 8vo., cloth, old style. Price 5s.

Studies of Sensation and Event.

Poems by EBENEZER JONES.

Edited, Prefaced, and Annotated by RICHARD HERNE SHEPHERD.

With Memorial Notices of the Author by SUMNER JONES and W. J. LINTON.

A new Edition. With Photographic Portrait of the Poet.

"This remarkable poet affords nearly the most striking instance of neglected genius in our modern school of poetry. His poems are full of vivid disorderly power."—D. G. ROSSETTI.

GEORGE REDWAY, YORK STREET, COVENT GARDEN.

In demy 8vo., elegantly printed on Dutch hand-made paper, and bound in parchment-paper cover. Price 1s.

The Scope and Charm of Antiquarian Study.

BY

JOHN BATTY, F.R.Hist.S.,

MEMBER OF THE YORKSHIRE ARCHÆOLOGICAL AND TOPOGRAPICAL ASSOCIATION.

"It forms a useful and entertaining guide to a beginner in historical researches."—*Notes and Queries*.

"The author has laid it before the public in a most inviting, intelligent, and intelligible form, and offers every incentive to the study in every department, including Ancient Records, Manorial Court-Rolls, Heraldry, Painted Glass, Mural Paintings, Pottery, Church Bells, Numismatics, Folk-Lore, etc., to each of which the attention of the student is directed. The pamphlet is printed on a beautiful modern antique paper, appropriate to the subject of the work."—*Brighton Examiner*.

"Mr. Batty, who is one of those folks Mr. Dobson styles 'gleaners after time,' has clearly and concisely summed up, in the space of a few pages, all the various objects which may legitimately be considered to come within the scope of antiquarian study."—*Academy*.

GEORGE REDWAY, YORK STREET, COVENT GARDEN.

*A few large-paper copies, with India proof portrait, in imperial 8vo.,
parchment.   Price 7s. 6d.*

An Essay on the Genius of George Cruikshank.

BY

"THETA" (WILLIAM MAKEPEACE THACKERAY).

With all the Original Woodcut Illustrations, a New Portrait of
CRUIKSHANK, etched by PAILTHORPE, and a Prefatory Note on
THACKERAY AS AN ART CRITIC, by W. E. CHURCH, Secretary of
the Urban Club.

———

" Thackeray's essay 'On the Genius of George Cruikshank,' reprinted from
the *Westminster Review*, is a piece of work well calculated to drive a critic of
these days to despair. How inimitable is its touch! At once familiar and
elegant, serious and humorous, enthusiastically appreciative, and yet just
and clear-sighted ; but, above all, what the French call *personnel*. It is not
the impersonnel reviewer who is going through his paces . . . it is Thackeray
talking to us as few can talk—talking with apparent carelessness, even
ramblingly, but never losing the thread of his discourse or saying a word too
much, nor ever missing a point which may help to elucidate his subject or
enhance the charm of his essay. . . . Mr. W. E. Church's prefatory note on
'Thackeray as an Art Critic' is interesting and carefully compiled."—*Westminster Review*, Jan. 15th.

"As the original copy of the *Westminster* is now excessively rare, this
reissue will, no doubt, be welcomed by collectors."—*Birmingham Daily Mail*.

"Not only on account of the author, but of the object, we must welcome
most cordially this production. Every bookman knows Thackeray, and will
be glad to have this production of his which deals with art criticism—a subject so peculiarly Thackeray's own."—*The Antiquary*.

"It was a pleasant and not untimely act to reprint this well-known
delightful essay. . . . the artist could have found no other commentator so
sympathetic and discriminating. . . . The new portrait of Cruikshank by
F. W. Pailthorpe is a clear, firm etching."—*The Artist*.

———

GEORGE REDWAY, YORK STREET, COVENT GARDEN.

In crown 8vo., cloth.   Price 7s. 6d.

Theosophy, Religion, and Occult Science.

BY

HENRY S. OLCOTT,

PRESIDENT OF THE THEOSOPHICAL SOCIETY.

WITH GLOSSARY OF EASTERN WORDS.

"This book, to which we can only allot an amount of space quite incom-
mensurate with its intrinsic interest, is one that will appeal to the prepared
student rather than to the general reader.   To anyone who has previously
made the acquaintance of such as Mr. Sinnett's 'Occult World,' and 'Esoteric
Buddhism,' or has in other ways familiarised himself with the doctrines of
the so-called Theosophical Society or Brotherhood, these lectures of Colonel
Olcott's will be rich in interest and suggestiveness.   The American officer is
a person of undoubted social position and unblemished personal reputation,
and his main object is not to secure belief in the reality of any 'phenomena,'
not to win a barren reputation for himself as a thaumaturgist or wonder-
worker, but to win acceptance for one of the oldest philosophies of nature
and human life—a philosophy to which of late years the thinkers of the
West have been turning with noteworthy curiosity and interest.   Of course,
should the genuineness of the phenomena in question be satisfactorily established, there would undoubtedly be proof that the Eastern sages to whom
Colonel Olcott bears witness do possess a knowledge of the laws of the
physical universe far wider and more intimate than that which has been
laboriously acquired by the inductive science of the West; but the theosophy
expounded in this volume is at once a theology, a metaphysic, and a socio-
logy, in which mere marvels, as such, occupy a quite subordinate and unimportant position.   We cannot now discuss its claims, and we will not pro-
nounce any opinion upon them; we will only say that Colonel Olcott's
volume deserves and will repay the study of all readers for whom the bye-
ways of speculation have an irresistible charm."—*Manchester Examiner.*

GEORGE REDWAY, YORK STREET, COVENT GARDEN.

Monthly, 2s.; Yearly Subscription, 20s.

The Theosophist:

A Magazine of Oriental Philosophy, Art, Literature and Occultism.

CONDUCTED BY

H. P. BLAVATSKY.

Vols. I. to VI. Now Ready.

"Theosophy has suddenly risen to importance. . . . The movement implied by the term Theosophy is one that cannot be adequately explained in a few words . . . those interested in the movement, which is not to be confounded with spiritualism, will find means of gratifying their curiosity by procuring the back numbers of *The Theosophist* and a very remarkable book call 'Isis Unveiled,' by Madame Blavatsky."—*Literary World.*

GEORGE REDWAY, YORK STREET, COVENT GARDEN.

NEW WORK BY JOHN H. INGRAM.

The Raven.

BY

EDGAR ALLAN POE.

With Historical and Literary Commentary. By JOHN H. INGRAM.

Crown 8vo., parchment, gilt top, uncut, price 6s.

"This is an interesting monograph on Poe's famous poem. First comes the poet's own account of the genesis of the poem, with a criticism, in which Mr. Ingram declines, very properly, we think, to accept the history as entirely genuine. Much curious information is collected in this essay. Then follows the poem itself, with the various readings, and then its after-history; and after these 'Isadore,' by Albert Pike, a composition which undoubtedly suggested the idea of 'The Raven' to its author. Several translations are given, two in French, one in prose, the other in rhymed verse; besides extracts from others, two in German and one in Latin. But perhaps the most interesting chapter in the book is that on the 'Fabrications.'"—*The Spectator.*

"There is no more reliable authority on the subject of Edgar Allan Poe than Mr. John H. Ingram . . . the volume is well printed and tastefully bound in spotless vellum, and will prove to be a work of the greatest interest to all students of English and American literature."—*The Publishers' Circular.*

GEORGE REDWAY, YORK STREET, COVENT GARDEN.

NEW REALISTIC NOVEL.

---

620 pages, handsomely bound.   Price 6s.

Leicester :

AN AUTOBIOGRAPHY.

BY

FRANCIS W. L. ADAMS.

"Even M. Zola and Mr. George Moore would find it hard to beat Mr. Adams's description of Rosy's death.   The grimly minute narrative of Leicester's schoolboy troubles and of his attempt to get a living when he is discarded by his guardian is, too, of such a character as to make one regret that Mr. Adams had not put to better use his undoubted, though undisciplined, powers."—*The Academy.*

"There is unquestionable power in 'Leicester.'"—*The Athenæum.*

GEORGE REDWAY, YORK STREET, COVENT GARDEN.

NEW BOOK BY MISS BAUGHAN.

The Handbook of Physiognomy.

BY

ROSA BAUGHAN

Demy 8vo., wrapper, Price 1s.

CONTENTS.—Chapter 1. "The Face is the Mirror of the Soul." II. The Forehead and Eyebrows.   III. The Eyes and Eyelashes. IV. The Nose.   V. The Mouth, Teeth, Jaw, and Chin.   VI. The Hair and the Ears.   VII. The Complexion.   VIII. Congenial Faces.   IX. The Signatures of the Planets on the Face.   X. Pathognomy.

GEORGE REDWAY, YORK STREET, COVENT GARDEN.

Small 4to., with Illustrations, bound in vegetable parchment.
Price 10s. 6d.

THE

Virgin of the World:

BY HERMES MERCURIUS TRISMEGISTUS.

A Treatise on INITIATIONS, or ASCLEPIOS; the DEFI-
NITIONS of ASCLEPIOS; FRAGMENTS of the
WRITINGS of HERMES.

TRANSLATED AND EDITED BY THE AUTHORS OF "THE PERFECT
WAY."

With an Introduction to "The Virgin of the World" by A. K.,
and an Essay on "The Hermetic Books" by E. M.

―――――

"It will be a most interesting study for every occultist to compare the
doctrines of the ancient Hermetic philosophy with the teaching of the
Vedantic and Buddhist systems of religious thought. The famous books of
Hermes seem to occupy, with reference to the Egyptian religion, the same
position which the Upanishads occupy in Aryan religious literature."—
The Theosophist, November, 1885.

―――――

GEORGE REDWAY, YORK STREET, COVENT GARDEN.

In preparation.

NEW TRANSLATION OF "THE HEPTAMERON."

THE "JOHN PAYNE" EDITION.

The Heptameron ;

OR,

Tales and Novels of Margaret, Queen of Navarre.

Now first done completely into English prose and verse, from the original French, by ARTHUR MACHEN.

With an Introduction by JOHN PAYNE, Translator of "The Poems of Master Francis Villon, of Paris," "The Book of the Thousand Nights and One Night," etc.

GEORGE REDWAY, YORK STREET, COVENT GARDEN.

One vol., crown 8vo., 400 pages. Price 6s.

A Regular Pickle :

How He Sowed his Wild Oats.

BY

HENRY W. NESFIELD.

"Mr. Nesfield's name as an author is established on such a pleasantly sound foundation that it is a recognised fact that, in taking up a book written by him, the reader is in for a delightful half-hour, during which his risible and humorous faculties will be pleasantly stimulated. The history of young Archibald Highton Tregauntly, whose fortunes we follow from the cradle to when experience is just beginning to teach him a few wholesome lessons, is as smart and brisk as it is possible to be."—*Whitehall Review.*

"It will be matter for regret if the brisk and lively style of Mr. Nesfield, who at times reminds us of Lever, should blind people to the downright wickedness of such a perverted career as is here described."—*Daily Chronicle.*

GEORGE REDWAY, YORK STREET, COVENT GARDEN.

Fourth Edition.   With Engraved Frontispiece.   In crown 8vo., 5s.

Cosmo de' Medici :

An Historical Tragedy.   And other Poems.

BY

RICHARD HENGIST HORNE,

Author of " Orion."

———

" This tragedy is the work of a poet and not of a playwright. Many of the scenes abound in vigour and tragic intensity. If the structure of the drama challenges comparison with the masterpieces of the Elizabethan stage, it is at least not unworthy of the models which have inspired it."—*Times.*

GEORGE REDWAY, YORK STREET, COVENT GARDEN.

Fcap. 8vo., parchment.

Tamerlane and other Poems.

BY

EDGAR ALLAN POE.

First published at Boston in 1827, and now first republished from a unique copy of the original edition, with a preface by RICHARD HERNE SHEPHERD.

———

Mr. Swinburne has generously praised " so beautiful and valuable a little volume, full of interest for the admirers of Poe's singular and exquisite genius."

GEORGE REDWAY, YORK STREET, COVENT GARDEN.

Just ready, in demy 8vo., choicely printed, and bound in Japanese parchment. Price 7s. 6d.

Primitive Symbolism

As Illustrated in Phallic Worship; or, The Reproductive Principle.

BY

The late HODDER M. WESTROPP.

With an Introduction by GENERAL FORLONG, Author of "Rivers of Life."

———

"This work is a *multum in parvo* of the growth and spread of Phallicism, as we commonly call the worship of nature or fertilizing powers. I felt, when solicited to enlarge and illustrate it on the sudden death of the lamented author, that it would be desecration to touch so complete a compendium by one of the most competent and soundest thinkers who have written on this world-wide faith. None knew better or saw more clearly than Mr. Westropp that in this oldest symbolism and worship lay the foundations of all the goodly systems we call religious."—J. G. R. FORLONG.

———

GEORGE REDWAY, YORK STREET, COVENT GARDEN.

In large crown 8vo. Price 3s. 6d.

Sithron, the Star Stricken.

Translated (*Ala bereket Allah*) from an ancient Arabic Manuscript.

BY

SALEM BEN UZÄIR, of Bassora.

———

"This very remarkable book, 'Sithron' . . . is a bold, pungent, audacious satire upon the ancient religious belief of the Jews. . . . No one can read the book without homage to the force, the tenderness, and the never-failing skill of its writer."—*St. James's Gazette.*

———

GEORGE REDWAY, YORK STREET, COVENT GARDEN.

Post free, price 3d.

The Literature of Occultism and Archæology.

Being a Catalogue of Books ON SALE relating to

Ancient Worships.
Astrology.
Alchemy.
Animal Magnetism.
Anthropology.
Arabic.
Assassins.
Antiquities.
Ancient History.
Behmen and the Mystics.
Buddhism.
Clairvoyance.
Cabeiri.
China.
Coins.
Druids.
Dreams and Visions.
Divination.
Divining Rod.
Demonology.
Ethnology.
Egypt.
Fascination.
Flagellants.
Freemasonry.
Folk-Lore.
Gnostics.
Gems.
Ghosts.
Hindus.
Hieroglyphics and Secret Writing.
Herbals.
Hermetic.
India and the Hindus.
Kabbala.
Koran.
Miracles.
Mirabilaries.

Magic and Magicians.
Mysteries.
Mithraic Worship
Mesmerism.
Mythology.
Metaphysics.
Mysticism.
Neo-platonism.
Orientalia.
Obelisks.
Oracles.
Occult Sciences.
Phallic Worship.
Philology.
Persian.
Parsees.
Philosophy.
Physiognomy.
Palmistry and Handwriting.
Phrenology.
Psychoneurology.
Psychometry.
Prophets.
Rosicrucians.
Round Towers.
Rabbinical.
Spiritualism.
Skeptics, Jesuits, Christians and Quakers.
Sibylls.
Symbolism.
Serpent Worship.
Secret Societies.
Somnambulism.
Travels.
Tombs.
Theosophical.
Theology and Criticism.
Witchcraft.

GEORGE REDWAY, YORK STREET, COVENT GARDEN.

In preparation.

The Praise of Ale ;

OR,

Songs, Ballads, Epigrams, and Anecdotes relating to

Beer, Malt, and Hops.

Collected and arranged by

W. MARCHANT.

☞ *Send for Prospectus.*

GEORGE REDWAY, YORK STREET, COVENT GARDEN.

In preparation.

Park's History and Topography of Hampstead.

Revised and brought down to the Present Time.

BY

EDWARD WALFORD, M.A.,

Editor of " Walford's Antiquarian."

☞ *Send for Prospectus.*

GEORGE REDWAY, YORK STREET, COVENT GARDEN.

REDWAYS SHILLING SERIES,

Nearly ready, Vol. IV.

Wellerisms.

EDITED BY

CHARLES KENT.

A collection of all the " good things " for which the Wellers, *père et fils*, are famous—a posy culled from the pages of *Pickwick* and *Master Humphrey's Clock.*

GEORGE REDWAY, YORK STREET, COVENT GARDEN.

Nearly ready.

The Curate's Wife.

A NOVEL.

BY

Mrs. J. E. PANTON,

Author of "Sketches in Black and White."

GEORGE REDWAY, YORK STREET, COVENT GARDEN.

Nearly ready.

The History of the Forty Vezirs;

OR,

The Story of the Forty Morns and Eves,

Written in Turkish by Sheykh-Zada, and now done into English by E. J. W. Gibb, M.R.A.S.

GEORGE REDWAY, YORK STREET, COVENT GARDEN.

In preparation.

Sea Songs and River Rhymes.

A SELECTION OF ENGLISH VERSE, FROM CHAUCER TO SWINBURNE.

EDITED BY

Mrs. DAVENPORT ADAMS.

With Etchings by Mackaness.

This is a Collection of Poems and Passages by English Writers on the subject of the Sea and Rivers, and covers the whole of the ground between Spenser and Tennyson. It includes numerous copyright Poems, for the reproduction of which the author and publishers have given their permission.

GEORGE REDWAY, YORK STREET, COVENT GARDEN.

Nearly ready.

Essays in the Study of Folk-Songs.

BY

THE COUNTESS EVELYN MARTINENGO-CESARESCO.

CONTENTS:

INTRODUCTION.
THE INSPIRATION OF DEATH IN FOLK-POETRY.
NATURE IN FOLK-SONGS.
ARMENIAN FOLK-SONGS.
VENETIAN FOLK-SONGS.
SICILIAN FOLK-SONGS.
GREEK SONGS OF CALABRIA.
FOLK-SONGS OF PROVENCE.
THE WHITE PATERNOSTER.
THE DIFFUSION OF BALLADS.
SONGS FOR THE RITE OF MAY.
THE IDEA OF FATE IN SOUTHERN TRADITIONS
FOLK-LULLABIES.
FOLK-DIRGES.

GEORGE REDWAY, YORK STREET, COVENT GARDEN.

Shortly will be published in 8vo. handsomely printed on antique paper, and tastefully bound. Price 1s. to Subscribers.

Pope Joan

(*THE FEMALE POPE*).

A Historical Study.   Translated from the Greek of Emmanuel Rhoïdis, with Preface by

CHARLES HASTINGS COLLETTE.

"The subject of POPE JOAN has not yet lost the interest which belongs to it, as a fact in the province of historical criticism."—*Dr. Döllinger.*

THE PLAYS OF GEORGE COLMAN THE YOUNGER.

The Comedies and Farces

OF
GEORGE COLMAN THE YOUNGER.

Now first collected and carefully reprinted from the Original Editions, with Annotations and Critical and Bibliographical Preface,

BY

RICHARD HERNE SHEPHERD.

In Two Volumes.

Some of these plays have become very scarce ; and of those which have kept the stage, the text has been more or less corrupted.

NEWLY-DISCOVERED POEM BY CHARLES LAMB.

Beauty and the Beast.

A Story in Verse for Children by CHARLES LAMB.   Now first reprinted from the Unique Original, with Preface and Notes

BY

RICHARD HERNE SHEPHERD.

Only 100 Copies printed.

GEORGE REDWAY, YORK STREET, COVENT GARDEN.

www.ingramcontent.com/pod-product-compliance
Lightning Source LLC
Chambersburg PA
CBHW020606030726
47497CB00007B/2106